Ashes of Roses

MARY JANE AUCH

Henry Holt and Company

New York

Henry Holt and Company, LLC, *Publishers since 1866*
115 West 18th Street, New York, New York 10011
www.henryholt.com

Henry Holt is a registered trademark of Henry Holt and Company, LLC
Copyright © 2002 by Mary Jane Auch. All rights reserved.
Distributed in Canada by H. B. Fenn and Company Ltd.

Library of Congress Cataloging-in-Publication Data
Auch, Mary Jane.
Ashes of roses / Mary Jane Auch.
p.   cm.
Summary: Sixteen-year-old Margaret Rose Nolan, newly arrived from Ireland,
finds work at New York City's Triangle Shirtwaist Factory shortly
before the 1911 fire in which 146 employees died.
1. Triangle Shirtwaist Company—Fire, 1911—Juvenile fiction.
[1. Triangle Shirtwaist Company—Fire, 1911—Fiction.
2. Immigrants—New York (N.Y.)—Fiction.   3. Irish Americans—Fiction.
4. Emigration and immigration—Fiction.   5. New York (N.Y.)—History—
1898–1951—Fiction.]   I. Title.
PZ7.A898 As 2002   [Fic]—dc21   2001051896

ISBN 0-8050-6686-1 / First Edition—2002
Printed in the United States of America on acid-free paper. ∞
1   3   5   7   9   10   8   6   4   2

*This book is dedicated
to the heroes of September 11, 2001—both
those who were lost and those who
fought to save them—and to the
indestructible spirit of the
people of New York.*

Ashes
of
Roses

1

There *was no sense* tryin' to sleep. This was the last night we'd be tossed by the waves in our narrow bunks. We were due to pull into New York Harbor at dawn, puttin' an end to the most unbearable two weeks of my life.

I shifted in my cot, tryin' to nudge my little sister, Bridget, over. She was barely four, and small for her age, but she took up more than her share of the narrow shelf we were supposed to call a bed. Ma had staked out a claim to four bunks in a row on the lower level when we first boarded the ship, but Bridget whimpered that she was lonely and moved into my bunk the first night. Next to us was Maureen, the middle sister, who made it clear from the beginnin' that she wasn't sharin' a bunk with anyone. I don't remember bein' that stubborn at twelve.

I heard poor little Joseph begin to whimper. He slept with Ma, although for the amount of sleepin' he did he might as well have kept his eyes wide open. The last few days especially, he was fussin' more time than he was quiet. I'd be glad to get off the ship so I wouldn't have to endure the comments of our fellow passengers, who were gettin' less patient with Joseph by the day. I loved my baby brother, but I wasn't so anxious to be around him myself.

I nudged Bridget over again, but the motion of the boat sent her rollin' right back to me. Finally, I gave up and fished for my shoes and shawl under my bunk. I decided to go up on the deck and see if any land was in sight. I tucked Bridget in with Maureen and climbed the ladder to the deck. A soft gray light filled the sky, and the wind made me pull my coat tighter around me. I wished we could have made this trip in the summer instead of February. We'd seen so little of sunshine, I'd almost forgotten what it looked like.

It had been two weeks ago that we set sail from Cork. As long as I could remember, Da had talked about comin' to America for a better life. So many people had left before us, it seemed the natural thing to do. As we pulled out of port, one man had shouted, "Will the last man out of Ireland please lock the door?" That brought a round of laughter from his friends, but we weren't more than an hour at sea before they were gulpin' pints of ale and singin' about wantin' to go back to dear old Ireland. Grandma Nolan had told Da that, no matter how much you wanted to leave, Ireland would tug on your heart until you returned. I thought she was just sayin' that to make him stay with her in Limerick, but maybe there was somethin' to it.

The deck was empty this last mornin' except for an old man who always seemed to be there, as if watchin' for land would bring it on sooner. He was leanin' on the rail, squintin' into the wind. "See that?" he asked.

I looked around to make sure he was talkin' to me. "See what?" I said.

"That dark shape over there? And another to the left of it? That's the Narrows. When we go through there, we'll be in New York Harbor."

"Ye mean it's land?" I asked. "I can't see anything at all."

As we moved closer, I could gradually make out what the man was talkin' about. There were other ships, too, but I couldn't tell if they were comin' or goin'. Other passengers were startin' to appear on deck now.

My heart beat fast as I crashed down the ladder to the steerage quarters. "Ma! Maureen! Get up! We can see New York. Come up on the deck."

Ma sat up and went into action. "Help me get shoes on the girls, Margaret Rose. And make sure all our things are packed into the two suitcases. Yer father has the trunk over in the men's quarters."

"But can't all this wait, Ma? I just want to see the city. I'll come right back to help ye."

All the talkin' had wakened other passengers. As they climbed out of their bunks, every inch of floor space filled with bodies. The first- and second-class passengers had their own compartments, but in steerage we were crammed like fish in a tin.

Maureen sat up and rubbed her eyes. "Where are we? Is this America?" She pulled on her shoes and headed for the ladder with laces floppin'.

"Stay right here," Ma said. "We need to gather our things. Maureen, take the large suitcase, and I'll carry the small one along with luggin' Joseph. Margaret Rose, you carry the feather bed and hang on to Bridget. There's goin' to be a great crush of people gettin' off this boat."

"But we're goin' to miss the Statue of Liberty," I protested. "I could've stayed on the deck, but I wanted ye all to see it."

"And see it we will," Ma said, "but we're not goin' up on the deck until I say we're ready. Now run a comb through yer hair, and yer sisters', too. I'll not have Uncle Patrick see ye lookin' like a bunch of ragamuffins."

Maureen and I were ready to jump out of our skins by the time Ma decided we were ready. We waited our turn in line. Maureen went up first; then Ma handed the large suitcase to her. It was my turn next. I was glad to be goin' up this ladder for the last time. All through the voyage, the boys would make a big fuss about lookin' up the girls' skirts as we climbed. They must have been pretty bored to get so worked up over a glimpse of bloomers.

Ma had the feather bed tied firmly in a tablecloth, but it was still bulky. I had struggled about halfway up the ladder when the ship began to tilt. I clung to the rung above me, but there was a ruckus behind Ma.

"Saints preserve us, we're sinkin'," a red-faced man shouted. He grabbed my shoulder and pulled me down from the ladder, then pushed ahead and climbed out to save himself. People were shovin' behind us.

"Go ahead, Margaret Rose," Ma said. "I'll be pushin' Bridget right up after ye."

"Are we sinkin'?" Bridget whined.

Ma gave her a boost. "I don't know, but I'd rather find out on the top deck than down here."

I turned to grab Bridget's hand. It was easy to keep track of Ma, because Joseph was howlin' like a banshee. We skidded down the narrow hallway packed in shoulder to shoulder with the other steerage passengers. The wall was tiltin' at a crazy angle, makin' it hard to sense which way was up. Were we really goin' to sink? Had we traveled all the way across the ocean only to be dumped like bilge into the harbor of New York?

"Stay together," Ma shouted. I could hear Maureen ahead of me with the big suitcase soundin' like a gong as it kept bumpin' the metal walls. If we had to jump overboard, I hoped she'd be sensible enough to leave it. Lord knows, there was little of any value in our belongin's. Certainly nothin' worth being anchored to the bottom of the harbor for.

There was a throng pushin' and shovin' at the last stairwell. "Margaret Rose, I'm frightened," Bridget wailed. I gathered her up in my arms, then shifted her to one hip so I could grab the iron railin' to keep my balance. When we finally came up out of steerage into the fresh air, I could hear the captain shoutin' over a bullhorn, "All passengers please move to the center of the boat."

There was no doubt that the deck was tilted, but I couldn't see that we were takin' on any water. The lifeboats hung in their places. The crew had made no move to load them. All of the passengers crowded together on the low side of the deck.

That's when I realized what the problem had been. We were just passin' the Statue of Liberty, and everyone had rushed to that side of the boat to see her.

The captain pleaded with the crowd again. "Ladies, gentlemen, please. Move away from the rail to the center." But nobody moved a muscle.

Ignorin' Ma's order to stay together, I put Bridget down, held tight to her hand, and pushed through the crowd. I finally squeezed into a spot by the rail and brought her around in front of me, where she could see through the iron mesh. I was afraid to lift her above the rail for fear I'd drop her overboard in my excitement.

There stood Lady Liberty, more beautiful than ever she'd appeared in the black-and-white pictures I'd seen. She was a lovely soft green in color, and the rosy sun gave a blush to her cheeks. I couldn't believe how big she was. She towered over the harbor like a giantess who had waded in from the ocean. The ship grew strangely silent. I saw tears in the eyes of the man next to me. It was February 18, 1911, the date that would mark the start of my new life.

My heart swelled with hope and fear at the same time. I had the feelin' that I was brought to America for a purpose. Somethin' important would happen to me here.

I remembered the words of the poem, "Give me your tired, your poor, your huddled masses . . ." Well, we were poor, all right, and after two weeks crammed into the bottom of a boat with Joseph screamin' his fool head off, we certainly qualified as tired, huddled masses.

"Here we are, America," I whispered. "We're just exactly what ye ordered."

2

Once we passed the Statue of Liberty, I tried to look for Da and Ma, but they were lost in a sea of hats. Poor Bridget was cryin' because she only came up to the belt buckles of most of the men. I was afraid she'd be trampled, so I lifted her on my hip, even though it made it harder to push through the people with the cumbersome feather bed. It was Da who found us, just as the ship was slippin' into the pier. He took Bridget in his strong arms so she could see over the crowd.

There was an announcement. "All first- and second-class passengers, go to B Deck for inspection, then disembark here. Steerage passengers will disembark and immediately board the ferry to Ellis Island."

"Are we first-class, Da?" Bridget asked.

Da shook his head. "No. We go to Ellis Island."

"But ye always call us yer first-class beauties," Bridget insisted.

Da kissed her cheek. "That ye are, lass, but the steamship company counts only the price of yer ticket. Someday, when we go back to visit Ireland, we'll travel first-class. After we've made our fortune in America."

I kept that in mind as we watched the fancy folks get off at the pier. We were herded like cattle onto the ferryboat, our feet touchin' America only for the time it took to walk from the ship's gangplank to the one leadin' to the ferry. Then it was off into the harbor again, this time headin' for a destination we feared.

We had heard many tales of Ellis Island—the place where the immigration officials decided whether or not ye were fit to enter America's gates. A person could be turned away for all sorts of things, especially sickness. I was thankful for the fact that we were healthy. Da always said, "We may be poor, but we have our health." Good health would be worth more than gold on Ellis Island.

I looked around at some of the other immigrants. One woman, pale as a ghost, held a sickly baby who seemed to struggle for each breath. I felt sorry for them. Surely they wouldn't make it past the medical inspection. There was a young man with a rackin' cough who didn't seem destined to become an American, either. I edged away from them. I wouldn't want to catch somethin' now that might keep me from gettin' into America.

Soon we could see Ellis Island up ahead. It looked like a confection, with its four domed turrets and dozens of arched windows edged with cream-colored bricks. It was hard to imagine that this pretty place could hold such terrible disappointment for some of the people on board with us.

We had a long time to worry about Ellis Island. There were two ferryboats steamin' ahead of us, and they landed first. We had to wait until all of their passengers were unloaded. It was two hours before we could set foot on land again. I spent the whole time avoidin' people who looked like they might be sick. There was no heat on the ferry, and a cold February wind blew across the water. By the time they let us off, my throat was already feelin' sore.

Finally, it was our turn. "Step lively, children," Da said. "Margaret Rose, mind ye keep a tight hold on Bridget. I don't want anyone gettin' lost."

The thought of losin' the family gave me a chill. I'd never seen so many people at once. I gripped Bridget's hand so tight she let out a yelp. Da took the feather bed to carry along with the trunk, so I grabbed the hem of his jacket with my other hand. I knew he wouldn't let anything happen to us.

We were given numbered tags and split into long lines. They separated the men from the women, then the women with small children. Joseph and Bridget went with Ma.

"How will we find each other again?" I asked, not wantin' to let go of Da.

"Just don't be losin' yer tag, whatever ye do," Da said. Maureen and I clung to each other as we moved forward in line.

"I'm scared," she whispered.

"Don't be a ninny," I said, tryin' to look brave, hopin' my tremblin' lower lip didn't give me away.

"There are so many people."

"There'll be even more when we get into New York, so get used to it."

When we neared the front of the line, an official-lookin' woman in a uniform came up to me. "Take down the top of your dress so the doctor can have a listen to your chest."

"But I've nothin' underneath," Maureen whispered. I was glad I wore a chemise under mine. I slipped out of my coat and dress top and held them around me until it was my turn.

The woman doctor was thin-lipped and stern. "Take a deep breath." The listenin' contraption was still warm from the last person. I tried to breathe as quietly as possible. What could she hear? Was there some little sound in my chest that could give me away as unhealthy and send me back to Ireland?

"A *deep* breath," she repeated.

This time, I obeyed. She listened, nodded, and waved me on ahead. I was poked and prodded by several more women, then allowed to button up my dress. I thought the worst was over, until I went into the last line. A man in a uniform told me to hold still. Then he pulled up my eyelid with a button-hook. It happened so quickly I didn't have time to cry out. But the second eye was worse, because I knew what to expect. I jerked my head back when I saw the hook comin'.

"You're just making this harder on yourself, girl," the examiner said, "and you're holding up the line."

"I'm sorry," I mumbled. I folded my arms tight around myself and tilted my head back obediently. He got a good grip on my lower lashes so I couldn't pull away. The hook hurt even more this time. When it was over, I emerged half stunned into the huge registry room.

"We have to find Ma and Da," I said, but Maureen wasn't there. Then I saw that she had moved several people behind in the line for the buttonhook examination. I shivered and turned away. That's when I saw Da sittin' on a bench. I ran to him. "Da, they just did the most terrible thing to me."

Da nodded. "The eye exam? 'Twas nasty, wasn't it? Patrick told me about it in a letter."

"Ye knew and ye didn't tell us?"

"Ah, so ye'd rather have worried about that exam comin' all the way across the ocean?"

"No, I guess not." I rubbed my eyes, where I could still feel the buttonhook. "But why do they do that?"

Da shrugged. "It's some disease they test for."

"But why don't they just tell ye to keep yer eyes open so they can look? I would gladly have done that. There was no need for the hook."

"Stop dwellin' on it, Margaret Rose. Just thank the good Lord ye passed. There's where ye'll be goin'." He pointed to a huge half-circle window that reached all the way to the two-story ceiling. At first I thought it was a picture in a frame, but then I realized I was lookin' for the first time at the great city of New York.

14

"Yer husband is waitin' for ye in that city," Da said, grinnin'.

I felt my face go red. "I'm a long way from lookin' for a husband, Da."

"Don't be so sure, Margaret Rose. There are more good Irish lads in the city of New York than in Dublin and Limerick put together."

I wasn't about to argue with Da, but I had no plans to marry at sixteen. A whole new world was stretchin' out before me, and I wanted a chance to savor it before I was weighed down with babies like Ma. She had had me when she was only seventeen. If we had stayed in Ireland, that would have been my fate, but I hoped there was somethin' else for me in America—somethin' more than bein' a wife and mother right away.

I looked up to see Ma comin' toward us with Bridget clingin' to her skirt and Joseph in her arms. He was thrashin' his head about and screamin' bloody murder. A man in uniform was with them.

Da stood up. "What's wrong?"

"You'll have to come with me, sir. I'm taking you to another room, where you can make arrangements."

"Arrangements? Arrangements for what?"

I couldn't help but notice the way the Americans talked. They spoke the English language, but it was hard to understand, and even harder on the ears. The man's "r"s sounded like a dog's growl, instead of Da's, which were soft like a purrin' cat.

The man led us into a side room. There were other families there, all lookin' as confused as we were. "Sit here and wait."

We all sat without protest, but as soon as the man left, Da gripped Ma's arm. "What the devil's goin' on?"

Ma's eyes were huge with fright. "It's Joseph. They won't let the poor babe into the country."

"That's nonsense," Da said. "Why would they keep out a baby? What harm could he do to anyone?"

Ma cuddled Joseph to her shoulder and stroked his head, but he was havin' none of it. "It's his eyes. They're sayin' he has some sort of infection. They told me the name. Nobody with this disease is allowed in the country."

"He's never had any trouble with his eyes. Let me see him." Da reached over and took Joseph into his lap.

"What's Joseph got writ on him?" Bridget asked. "Read me what it says."

Someone had chalked the letters "E C" on his little wool jacket. "It's not a word," I whispered in her ear. "It's just letters." I noticed several other people in the room with the same chalkmarks on their clothes. They all looked perfectly normal to me.

Bridget's voice got higher. "What's happened to Joseph's eyes? They're all squinty."

"She's right," I said. "He wasn't like that before. What did they do to him?"

Ma's hand trembled as she reached over and smoothed back Joseph's hair. "It's the drops. They pried his eyes wide open and squeezed somethin' in from a bottle. Must have stung like the very devil."

"I'll see about this." Da handed Joseph back to Ma. "There wasn't a thing wrong with the boy's eyes till they messed with him. Tried to blind the poor babe, they did."

He started out of the room.

"Michael, please don't go. They told us to stay here and wait."

Da didn't listen to her. I followed him as far as the door and watched as he marched directly to the head of the eye-examination line. The examiner pointed to the end of the line. They argued for a few minutes, with Da wavin' his arms, gesturin' toward us. I didn't need to hear the words to know that Da wasn't winnin' the argument. Then he went over to the next examiner, and the hand-wavin' started anew. I leaned out of the doorway so I could see him talkin' to three more people at desks, gettin' more agitated with each one. Finally, a man took him by the elbow and brought him over to our room. I ducked back to the bench so Da wouldn't know I'd been spyin' on him.

"What did they say, Michael?" Ma asked. "Is it all settled, then?"

Da didn't have to answer. From the look on his face, I knew that little Joseph Nolan was not about to become an American. And if he couldn't, I had a gnawin' fear that none of us could.

3

"It's no use," Da said. "They say anybody who's got the trachoma doesn't get into America. That's the law."

"Is it catchin'?" I edged away from Joseph, thinkin' of the many times I had held him. "He seemed fine before." Of course, he'd been bawlin' his way clear across the ocean, but that was just Joseph.

Da rubbed his forehead. "The man said most people come in here not knowin' they have it."

"Can they make him better?" I asked. "Can we . . ."

Da didn't let me finish. "Stop with yer questions, girl. How's a man to think?"

I watched as the people who were behind us in line moved ahead to the next holdin' pen. I could hear a ferry blast its horn.

"So we all return now?" Ma asked. "After everything it took to get here, now they ship all of us back?"

Da shook his head. "Not all of us. Joseph's the only one. The rest of us checked out fine."

Ma pulled Joseph close to her. "Have ye lost yer mind, Michael? I'm not givin' up my baby. If Joseph goes back, we all go back."

Da's head snapped up. "And use what to pay for the passage?"

Ma clutched at Da's sleeve. "But we had some money left after we paid for the tickets."

"Not enough."

"Surely there's a less expensive ship. One we could all afford to take."

"Good Lord, Margaret, if we had any cheaper quarters they'd be draggin' us across the sea at the end of a tow rope."

Ma was sobbin' now, her face buried in Joseph's shoulder. I patted her back, makin' sure not to get too close to Joseph. Then I saw Maureen standin' in the registry room, lookin' around with a panicked expression on her face. In all the fuss about Joseph we'd forgotten her. I ran out to get her.

Maureen looked relieved when she saw me. "Where did everybody go?"

I pointed to our family sittin' in the side room.

"Why's Joseph takin' on so?"

"They put somethin' in his eyes. He's got the trachoma."

"What's that?" Maureen looked past me. "What's got Ma so upset?"

"Whatever it is, it's bad enough to keep Joseph out of America. He has to go back."

Maureen just stared at me for a few seconds; then her eyes narrowed. I knew that look. Maureen's temper was worse than Da's. "Oh, no, they don't. Nobody can make me go back. I passed the examination. I'm goin' to be an American and that's all there is to it."

"Don't get so worked up. Joseph's the only one they're holdin' back. Da says there's not enough money to send us all back to Ireland."

"Well, a baby can't cross the ocean by himself. Did ye think of that? Somebody will have to go with him."

Maureen was right. Da had to be here to support us with his wages, and Ma would need to care for Bridget and bring in some extra money with her sewin'. Maureen was too young to care for Joseph all the way back over the ocean. So there was only one logical person. Me. But they couldn't make me do it. I'd dive off Ellis Island and swim for New York before I'd get on a boat bound for Ireland. We had nothin' back in Ireland but cranky old Grandma Nolan. And there wasn't a boy in Limerick I'd want for a husband. I ran back to the family just in time to hear the plan Da had come up with.

"I'll take the boy back to my mother," he said. "She'll be happy to care for him."

Da was goin'? I didn't have to go back? And Grandma Nolan would be happy to get Joseph? Not likely. As far as I'd seen, she was never happy about anything.

"I'll have to work a while to get the money to book my passage back to America," Da continued. "If the boy's eyes are clear by then, I'll bring him. If not, he can stay with my mother. Lord knows, she's raised enough Nolan boys to make a good job of it."

"Joseph is not one of yer mother's Nolan boys," Ma sobbed. "He's my son, not hers." But Da wasn't listenin'. He was busy countin' out the money he had.

I once heard Grandma Nolan say that children should be raised like cabbages—they'd do just fine if ye kept pullin' out the weeds. Poor Joseph was spoiled, bein' the youngest, and headstrong. Grandma would have a good deal of weed-pullin' to do on him, I suspected.

There was another blast from the ferry whistle. An old woman sat on the bench across from us with her belongin's, cryin' as her family kissed her goodbye and left her. There was an "H" chalked on her coat. Did that stand for a broken heart? What kind of country would break up families this way?

Ma was near hysterical now. "I can't abandon my baby. He's barely weaned."

"He's weaned almost six months now, Margaret." Da jutted out his chin, but his eyes had the shimmer of tears in them. "I've reasoned this out, and there's no other way. Think of yer daughters. There's no life for them in Ireland."

"They'll marry and have children," Ma said. "It was good enough for me."

"But not for me," I whispered, not quite brave enough to say the words for all to hear.

Ma rose from the bench. "What about yer dreams for yer only son in America? Ye're givin' up on him?"

"Joseph will come to America one day, but this isn't his time." He stood up. "Now, take the girls and get in line."

Ma clutched at Da's lapels. "I don't know how to make my way here alone, Michael."

"Ye'll not be alone. Ye'll be with my brother and his family. And Margaret Rose is almost full-grown. She'll be a help to ye." He pushed some money and a folded piece of paper into her hand. "I'm leavin' myself just enough money for the return trip. Give the rest to Patrick. Here's his address. I'll send ye a letter as soon as I get there. And be sure to write and let me know how ye're doin'."

Da unstrapped the trunk, pulled out a few things for himself and Joseph, and packed them in the smaller suitcase.

The examiner came into the room. "We'll have to separate you now. Who is going back with the child?"

"I'll be takin' him," Da said.

"All right, then, follow me."

Da kissed us each in turn. "Be strong," he whispered to me. "Yer ma needs ye now."

"Maybe Ma should be the one to take Joseph," I whispered back.

Da shook his head. "Leave it be, Margaret Rose. Yer ma wasn't so keen on comin' here in the first place. If she goes back . . ." He didn't finish the sentence.

Da tried to pull the squallin' Joseph from Ma's arms, but Joseph hung on like a burdock. The poor babe was tired and sick. All he wanted was his ma, and I couldn't stand to watch the struggle. I stepped behind Ma and pried Joseph's little fists away from the collar of her coat.

As Da wrenched Joseph away, Ma followed him out into the registry room, but I caught her around her waist and held tight. "Don't take my baby!" Ma wailed. "Please, Michael, he needs me."

The examiner cleared his throat and looked away. He had a sad expression on his face, as if he'd watched this scene play out a hundred times before.

"Margaret Rose," Da said, his voice hoarse. "Help yer mother." He had tears rollin' down his cheeks.

I knew he was askin' for help for himself, not Ma. "Please, Ma," I said, pressin' my cheek against hers. "Nothin' can be done. Ye're only makin' it worse fer all of us." I knew I was doin' the right thing, but it felt as if I was breakin' apart all the links that held our family together.

I don't know if it was my words or my holdin' her back that got through to Ma. All of a sudden she stopped strugglin' and sagged against me. Then her piercin' scream echoed at me from all corners of the huge room, like arrows goin' through my body.

The last thing I saw was Joseph reachin' his little arms over Da's shoulder, his eyes wide with the shock of betrayal. I hadn't even kissed my poor brother goodbye.

4

❧ *We huddled together* in the registry room, tryin' to comfort Ma, though she was near inconsolable. People walked around us, as if we were just a pile of luggage. It seemed forever before Ma quieted down enough to be reasoned with.

"Joseph will be fine," I said. "He'll probably be comin' back with Da in just a few weeks."

"Two weeks each way for the passage," Ma said, sniffling. "In between, another month or two earnin' the fare. Babies forget. My own son won't know me when we meet again."

Ma pulled out her handkerchief and sobbed into it until a woman in uniform tapped her gently on the shoulder. "You must move on now. Follow me, please." She took us across the registry room and pointed to a long bench surrounded by high railings and a chain fence. "Wait here until your name is called."

We settled ourselves and our goods and looked up to find ourselves facin' a bench full of people on the other side of our pen. Behind them was another pen, and another, stretchin' as far as we could see, all crammed with people.

Maureen folded her arms and slid down in the seat. "We've done enough waitin'. I want to see New York."

"Hush," Ma said. "We might miss hearin' our name."

So we sat in silence, jumpin' every time a person came by callin' out names. They were speakin' in all kinds of languages, recitin' names unlike any I'd ever heard. It wasn't long before the words melted into each other, and I was afraid I wouldn't recognize our name even if I heard it loud and clear.

The people around us looked foreign. Not Irish, for sure. Most had brown or black hair, dark skin, and odd clothing. The women wore full, printed skirts with shawls and kerchiefs. Even the tiniest of the girls were bundled up like little old ladies. Some of the men wore strange fur hats that looked like overturned flowerpots. I tried to eavesdrop on their conversations, but the words made no sense. The only thing we all had in common was the fear on our faces.

I stood up and looked around. Though there had been two thousand of us on the boat from Ireland, I didn't see a familiar face now, or even the pale skin and blue eyes of an Irishman. In the time we'd lost with the business over Joseph, it seemed our whole ship had been passed through Ellis Island.

My heart felt like a fist in my chest. Poor little Joseph. Would Da be able to comfort him? I felt guiltily grateful that Ma had stayed with us. Though Da was the head of the family, it was Ma who could make me feel better when I was sick or frightened. I had the feelin' I'd be needin' that comfort in the comin' weeks. As much as I wanted the adventure of comin' to America, I could already feel myself longin' for the familiar streets of Limerick and the sight of Thomond Bridge over the River Shannon.

Ma jumped suddenly to her feet. "Nolan! That's us." We hastily gathered up our goods and half carried, half dragged them over to the registration desk. Ma had to carry Bridget, because she'd fallen asleep.

We arrived at the desk at the same time as another family.

"It was our name they called," Ma said. "Just now. Nolan."

The man looked up from his book. "They called Cohen," he said. "Go back and wait your turn. And listen more carefully this time."

Ma's face flushed red. "Come, children." When we got back to our seats, another family had taken them.

Ma wanted to stand there, but a guard made us move along. "Find seats. Everyone must be seated," he said. "We can't have people milling around."

"We're not millin', we're standin' still," Maureen snapped.

"Take those seats over there." The guard pointed way back in the room.

"But here are some closer," Ma offered.

The guard pointed again. "Over there, and be quick about it."

We dragged our luggage back to where the guard told us to go. "That's the kind of trouble yer smart mouth is goin' to get us in America," Ma said to Maureen. "I don't want to hear any of yer sass when we meet yer Uncle Patrick. Is that understood?"

Maureen sat down with a thud, refusin' to look at Ma. Now we were farther from where the names were bein' called out, so we had to strain our ears to hear. When we finally heard "Nolan," we all jumped off the bench as if shot from a cannon.

We went to a different desk this time. A man with glasses on the end of his nose looked up. "The family of Michael Nolan?"

"Yes," Ma said.

"Where's the husband? Michael Nolan? Are you here?" His voice rose. "Michael Nolan!"

"He's gone back with our little brother, Joseph," I said. "He had the trachoma."

Ma gave me a look that said I had revealed too much of our business. Da had told us to answer the questions and not volunteer anything extra.

The examiner fixed his sharp gaze on me. "There's no man of the family?"

"There was a man of the family," Maureen said. She was about to say more, but Ma stuck her in the ribs with her elbow.

"I can't let you in the country with no means to support yourselves."

"I can sew," Ma blurted out. Then she cleared her throat. "I'm a seamstress. A good one."

The man shook his head. "You can't support a family on the pittance one woman can bring in with her sewing."

"My oldest daughter is a seamstress, too."

Ma's elbow wiped the surprised look from my face. Though I'd done a bit of mendin' for the family, I couldn't be called a seamstress by any stretch of the imagination. Still, I knew better than to give myself away.

The man leaned back and studied us for a second. "All right. That's better. Let's get on with the questions. Your name?"

"Margaret Nolan."

"Your birthplace?"

Ma hesitated, not understandin' his accent.

"Where were you born?"

"Oh. Ireland. Limerick."

"Your destination?"

"New York City."

"Where will you be staying? Do you have any family here?"

"Yes." Ma pulled a wrinkled piece of paper with Uncle Patrick's address from her pocket and smoothed it out on the desk.

"Have they been notified of your arrival?"

"Yes," Ma said. "My husband's brother is expectin' us. He'll see to us until my husband comes back."

The man shook his head and mumbled, "They always think the husbands are coming back."

Ma's face went red from anger this time.

The examiner carried on with the questions, spittin' them out in rapid fire like bullets. He wanted to know Ma's occupation, if she'd ever been in jail, and if she was an anarchist, whatever that was. Then he asked how much money she had.

"I don't know . . . My husband gave me . . . I haven't counted it." She pulled out the mess of bills and coins and started to hand it to him, but he just waved it away and wrote somethin' down.

"Do you have a job waiting for you in this country?" We all knew this was a trick question. The law didn't allow a person to have a job lined up before comin' here. But they didn't want immigrants who could become a burden on the state, so, if they thought it unlikely that ye'd get a job, they'd ship ye back. That didn't make any sense to me. A person could lose either way.

I held my breath as Ma said, "There is no job waitin' for me, but I have the skills to find work."

It was my turn to be questioned next. The examiner seemed impatient, ready to be done with us. "Name?"

"Rose Nolan," I said.

"It's Margaret Rose," Ma corrected.

The man didn't look up. "Rose or Margaret Rose? Which is it?"

"Rose," I repeated, assertin' my new American independence. I didn't like havin' to share the name Margaret with Ma, and "Rose" suited me. I wanted a more unusual name. In Ireland, half the girls I knew had double names that started with Margaret or Mary.

The man asked me the same questions he had asked Ma. When he got to the part about my occupation, I remembered to say I was a seamstress, even though the words almost stuck in my throat.

America didn't care if Bridget and Maureen were anarchists or criminals or seamstresses. Only their names and birthplaces were important.

"All right, I have one more name here. Son, Joseph Nolan. Is that the child who was unfit?"

Ma nodded, unable to speak. I bristled at the word "unfit," but a sudden thought hit me. If this man still had Da's and Joseph's names on the list, we might have been able to sneak Joseph through. We could have rubbed the chalkmarks from his jacket, left the holdin' room, and just brazened it out. With so many people comin' through here, who would have known? It was a good thing the examiner couldn't read my mind, or he would have marked me down as a criminal—another Nolan unfit to enter the country.

The examiner stamped a paper and handed it to Ma. "Take your things down the center flight of stairs and out to the pier to the place called 'the kissing post.' Your family should be waiting for you there. The ferry will take you into the city."

Maureen grabbed one trunk handle and I took the other. I was still in charge of the feather bed, which seemed to be gettin' heavier by the minute. We had to pass through a small metal wicket to leave the room. I had thought the gateway to America would be more grand than this, with trumpets and fireworks to usher us in. Instead, nobody bothered to look up and take notice as the Nolan women passed though the gate to a new life. But it didn't matter to me. We were in America at last, and I could hear the trumpets in my own head.

5

As we descended the staircase, I noticed that all of the people to our left had chalkmarks on their coats. The people in our line were goin' straight out onto the pier, but those to the right were bein' sent through another door that led back into the building.

Maureen and I struggled to carry the trunk between us. "I can hardly remember what Uncle Patrick looks like," I said.

"Ye weren't much older than Bridget when we last saw him," Ma said. "I think I'll know him, though."

"What does his wife look like?"

"That I couldn't tell ye. He never wrote much about her. She has two daughters somewhere near your age, I'd guess."

When we got out on the pier, we set down the trunk so we could look around for a couple with two grown daughters. There was such a swarm of people, all embracin' and kissin'. As soon as people greeted their relatives, they went to stand in line for the ferry that was headed back to New York.

There was a sudden ruckus near us, between a guard and a young mother with a babe in arms and a toddler clingin' to her skirts. "Madam, I told you before, you're not allowed to go into the city until your relatives come get you."

"But they maybe not know we here," the woman pleaded. "I go meet them in New York."

The guard took her arm. "We sent a telegram telling them to come here to pick you up. You must wait for them. An unescorted woman is not allowed to leave Ellis Island unless her relatives come for her."

"But if they no come?"

"Then you'll have to go back where you came from. I'm sorry. It's the law."

Ma grabbed Bridget and picked up the suitcase. "Come, children." She headed for the middle of the biggest crowd.

Maureen and I struggled to keep up with her. When we got in the midst of all the people, she smiled at a man next to her, then turned to hug me. "It's so good to see you again. My, how ye've grown."

"But, Ma, where is Uncle—"

She cut me off with a laugh. "Ah, 'tis kind of ye to say so."

"He's not here, is he?" I whispered into her ear. "We're goin' to sneak off Ellis Island and into New York, aren't we?"

Ma threw back her head and laughed again. "That's exactly right! I knew ye'd understand."

She smiled again at the man next to her and walked close behind as he and his relatives headed toward the ferry.

Maureen tugged on my coat sleeve. "Is that Uncle Patrick? Don't I get to meet him?"

I grabbed her elbow. "Keep yer mouth shut," I whispered. "Just follow us and look happy to be in America."

By some miracle, Maureen understood somethin' was wrong and did as she was told.

Ma and I stayed close to the man and his family, noddin' and smilin' when one of them looked at us. The line moved quickly, and we soon reached the gangplank. Just as we got there, one of the men loadin' the ferry pulled the rope across, blockin' us from gettin' on. Our pretend family had made it on board.

"Please, sir," I said, pointin' toward the ferry. "Our dear uncle . . . We mustn't be separated."

The man pulled back the rope. "Oh, sorry. Go ahead."

As soon as we made our way onto the crowded lower deck, the men pulled up the gangplank. The one who had let us through unwound the heavy rope from its mooring and threw it to his partner on board. The engine rumbled, and we moved away from the pier. We had escaped Ellis Island!

Ma found a spot for us on the outside deck, near the front of the boat. It was one of the few empty places, because there was no protection from the wind there. We put the feather bed on top of our luggage, then sat snuggled together.

"What we just did was not right," Ma said.

Maureen looked puzzled. "What did we do?"

Bridget started to whimper. Ma pulled her shawl around her. "We were supposed to wait for Uncle Patrick to come get us before we left Ellis Island."

"Why didn't he come?" Maureen asked.

"I don't know," Ma said. "Maybe he just doesn't know we're here. But I have his address. We'll find him instead."

"Then we haven't done anythin' wrong," Maureen said. "It's a silly rule to have to wait for your relatives."

"We're new in this country," Ma snapped. "We will obey all the rules here, even the silly ones. It's just that I was afraid if we didn't leave right away . . ." Her voice trailed off.

"Ma was afraid we would be sent back," I said. "We heard a guard talkin' to a woman with two small children. Nobody had come for her."

"But what if she had no money?" Maureen asked. "Who would pay for her ticket?"

"I don't know," Ma said. "If America wants to get rid of ye bad enough, I suppose the government would pay yer way back."

"Then we all could have gone home with Da and Joseph?" Maureen persisted. "The government would have paid for us?"

Ma was silent, but from the expression on her face, I knew she was thinkin' we might have lost an opportunity to be together as a family. That meant more to Ma than bein' in America. Wherever her husband and children were, that was home to Ma. I was grateful the subject hadn't come up before now. I didn't like havin' the family split up, but I had waited a long time to get to America, and I was goin' to be an American no matter what.

Ma was so lost in thought, I was afraid she was plannin' to remain on the ferry for its return trip to Ellis Island in the hopes of findin' Da and gettin' us all shipped off to Ireland.

"I think they'd only do that for criminals and such," I said.

"Do what?" Maureen asked.

"Pay to send ye back where ye came from," I said, watchin' Ma's face. "They know we're harmless. They wouldn't put out good money to be rid of the likes of us."

Ma considered this for a moment, then nodded. "This is the last we will speak of the matter. We'll find yer uncle and be welcomed into his home. And that's the end of it."

I looked over Maureen's head at the city that loomed ahead of us. I'd never seen buildings this tall. It was hard to picture how people could have cozy homes in such a place. Did they all live stacked on top of each other like logs in a woodpile? I wondered if Uncle Patrick and his wife would be glad to see us. Was it possible that he knew we were here and didn't come on purpose? I shook the thought from my mind.

And poor Da. Had he already started back to Ireland? I wished I had said a better goodbye. I squinted, searchin' along the rails of the ferries, tugboats, and steamers in the harbor. I was hopin' to see Da's face so I could wave goodbye to him, but they were all strangers.

It was a short trip to New York. Before we had time to think about what was happenin' to us, the ferry landed and we were spewed down the gangplank with the other passengers. We searched the crowd for Uncle Patrick, but he wasn't there.

Suddenly two men with a handcart came runnin' over to us. "You want help with your luggage?" the tall one asked. Without waitin' for an answer, he wrenched the trunk away from Ma and me.

"No!" I shouted. "Give it back." Da had told us we were never to let our luggage out of our sight. He wouldn't even leave anythin' in the luggage room at Ellis Island, because he'd been told things were stolen from there.

The short man wrestled with Maureen for the suitcase, but she kicked him in the shins.

"Brat!" he yelled.

By now a crowd was gatherin' around us. "The ladies told you they didn't need yer help," a voice said with what I could swear was an Irish accent. Then we saw him— a policeman who could have come straight from the streets of Limerick. The men dropped our luggage and ran.

The policeman tipped his hat. "Officer Jack Connelly at yer service, ladies. Ye were wise not to go with them thugs. They work for the boardin' houses around here. Once they have yer luggage, they'll charge ye a big fee for storage even if ye don't want to stay in their filthy houses. Where would ye be goin'?"

"My husband's brother." Ma took out the paper and handed it to him.

"Twelfth Street near Third Avenue. Easiest way to get there is on the Third Avenue el. Ye'll need to buy . . ." He looked at Bridget and smiled, then pulled some coins out of his pocket and handed them to Ma. "I don't usually do this, but she looks just like my youngest. Put these coins into the turnstile. Then ye'll take the uptown train and get off at the . . ." He counted on his fingers, mumblin' the names of the stations. "It's the ninth stop, I think. The Ninth Street station. It'll be a short walk from there."

"That's easy to remember," Maureen said. "Ninth Street, ninth stop."

Officer Connelly laughed. "That it is." He pointed to a train track that appeared for all the world to be hangin' from the sky. "Good luck to ye," he said, "and welcome to these United States."

I couldn't believe it. We'd been in New York for only a few minutes and already we'd been given some money. The stories we'd heard back in Ireland were true. The streets in America were indeed paved with gold.

6

We weren't the only ones draggin' luggage up the stairs to the elevated railroad. There seemed to be a steady stream of people comin' from the Ellis Island ferries. We waited by the tracks, wonderin' what manner of train would be ridin' on rails so high up. We heard it before we saw it come thunderin' into the station. Bridget started to wail, so Ma picked her up and had Maureen and me carry the feather bed and trunk. A man stopped to help us get all our luggage on the train. I could tell he wasn't the sort to run off with our goods, but Ma made sure he didn't touch a thing.

We stayed close to the door. Ma didn't let us get settled in on the seats that ran along both sides of the car, because she was afraid we wouldn't be able to get up and out when our stop came. This meant we were jostled by people both gettin' on and gettin' off for the eight stops before ours.

Ma kept shoutin' orders at us. "Girls, hold on to those trunk handles so ye don't get separated. And, Margaret Rose, make sure to keep the feather bed in yer other hand. I'll carry Bridget and the suitcase. And, Margaret Rose, when we get off, grab on to my skirt so we stay together."

"I've only got two hands, Ma," I said. I wanted to remind her about my new name, but I knew this wasn't the time.

"Stop number nine. This is us!" Ma shouted. I'm sure she would have leapt to the platform before the train came to a stop if the doors hadn't held her back. As soon as the doors slid open, we all tumbled out. Then we found our way down to the street.

At the bottom of the stairs we looked around, not sure of which way to go. We'd only been standin' there for a few seconds when a policeman approached us. "Would ye be needin' some help?" he asked. Were all the policemen in America from Ireland?

Ma seemed to calm at the sound of his voice. She pulled out the slip of paper. "Yes, Officer. We're lookin' for this address, if ye'd be so kind."

The policeman pointed out the direction we should go, only three blocks away. Ma thanked him, and we gathered up our luggage for the last time.

When we reached the stoop in front of the building, Ma lined us up and began pokin' and primpin' us, straightenin' out collars and smoothin' down stray locks of hair with spit. "Now, mind ye behave yerselves. We'll be the guests of

Uncle Patrick until yer father returns. There'll be no need of commentin' on things that might not be exactly to yer likin'. Is that clear?"

"Yes, Ma," we all mumbled, even Bridget.

"And ye'll stand up straight like proper ladies, use yer napkins instead of yer sleeves to wipe yer mouths at meals, and don't ye be sayin' a word unless somebody speaks to ye first."

"Yes, Ma," we chorused again.

"And I'll beat the stuffin' out of . . ."

"Ma, please!" I said. "It's cold. We'll all be good. Ye don't have to mention every possible way we might get into trouble."

Ma gave me a sharp look, then laughed. I wondered if her lecture to us was as much a way to postpone havin' to go in as anything. She almost seemed nervous at the prospect of meetin' Uncle Patrick's family, which seemed odd, because she and Da had always spoken of him with such fondness. "All right," she said, lookin' over the names on the mailboxes. "Here 'tis. Nolan. Number seven. Look at that, will ye? Our name written out plain as day all the way over here in America."

I saw her hand shake as she pushed open the inner door. There was a small foyer with little black and white tiles on the floor, washed so clean the white ones almost sparkled. The stairway had a polished wooden banister that wound its way up as far as we could see. "I hope we don't have to climb seven floors," I said.

"Why don't we leave the trunk here and let Uncle Patrick come down for it?" Maureen offered.

Ma picked up one end of the trunk and motioned for me to do the same. "Nonsense. If he's kind enough to share his home with us, the very least we can do is carry our own goods to his door."

There were three apartments on each floor, so we only had to climb two flights of stairs to reach number seven. Ma gave us each another goin' over before she knocked.

A tall blond woman opened the door just a few inches. There was a small crease between her eyebrows, and she did not smile. "Yah?" she said.

"Are you Mrs. Nolan?" Ma asked.

The woman nodded suspiciously. A small towheaded boy squeezed in front of her and peered at us.

"I'm Margaret," Ma said. "And these are me children."

"I'm sorry," the woman said, and would have closed the door right in our faces if Uncle Patrick hadn't come up behind her and stopped the door with his hand. "Who is it, Elsa?"

"It's nobody. It's just . . ."

"Patrick!" Ma called out. "It's Margaret. Michael's wife."

He opened the door all the way, stared at us for a second, then let out a whoop and swept Ma into his arms.

"Margaret! I can't believe ye're here! Where's Michael?"

"He had to go back with the baby," Ma said. "The dear child had the trachoma, the infection of the eyes."

The small boy had started to edge his way toward us, but Elsa pulled him back when she heard the mention of trachoma, knowin', no doubt, how contagious it was.

Uncle Patrick picked up the trunk. "Well, don't be standin' in the hall. We were right in the middle of dinner. Come set down yer things and join us."

Uncle Patrick led us through a small parlor and into the next room, which held a table, buffet, and china closet. Two young women sat at the table and got up when we entered the room.

"Ye've already met me wife, Elsa, and these are her two daughters, Trudy and Hildegarde, and our son, Friedrich."

Friedrich Nolan, I thought. Some good old Irish name that is!

When Ma introduced us, I had to correct her on my name. She just smiled and nodded. "Oh, yes. Rose. Her new American name."

Trudy looked older than me, with blond hair wrapped in a braid around her head and a mouth pursed up like she was holdin' sewin' pins in it. Hildegarde was somewhere between Maureen's age and mine, a younger, softer version of her sister. Though the expression on her face wasn't exactly friendly, she at least looked at us with interest. Both girls wore the fashionable new Gibson Girl shirtwaists that we had seen in a magazine at home. The delicate white fabric made my brown homespun dress look like a burlap feed-sack.

Ma was so happy to be among family again, she went around the room huggin' them one by one. Everybody was smilin', but I noticed that Elsa and each of her daughters pulled back a bit just before Ma grabbed them.

Uncle Patrick brought extra chairs to the table. Elsa had recovered some manners and set out plates and cups for us. Then she came back from the kitchen with the worst-smellin' concoction I had ever run into and dropped a big gray dollop of it onto each of our plates.

Bridget wrinkled her nose. "What is that?"

Uncle Patrick laughed. "It's sauerkraut, made out of cabbage. Ye never had that in the old country, did ye?"

We hadn't eaten all day, so I was hungry enough to take a bite. The smell wasn't the worst of it, though. It had a bitter taste that made me want to spit it out rather than swallow, but I knew Ma would light into me good if I tried a trick like that. I chewed my mouthful for a long time, then, finally, managed to get it down. I remembered the sweet boiled cabbage we had at home and wondered how on earth anyone could get a cabbage to behave like this. Hildegarde passed me the breadboard with thick slices of black bread. I took it gratefully and let the dark-rye taste drown out the sauerkraut.

Ma was so excited she ate the sauerkraut without noticin' what an abomination it was. She carried on a conversation with Uncle Patrick about all the people he used to know in Limerick. She didn't seem to notice the looks that were flyin' around the table. Trudy was havin' a silent conversation with her mother. There were no words, but her eyes asked, "Who are these people, and how soon can we be rid of them?"

Uncle Patrick sat back in his chair. "I can't believe ye're here. I knew Michael wanted to come someday, but I had no idea it would be this soon."

"Ye mean ye didn't expect us?" Ma asked, her eyes widening. "Ye didn't get Michael's letter? He sent it just before we left Ireland."

"The mails can take weeks from the old country," Uncle Patrick said. "No, we had no idea. Did he arrange for a place to stay?"

Ma's face turned red. She was speechless just long enough for Maureen to blurt out, "Da said ye'd let us stay here until he came back. That's all right, isn't it?"

Ma's elbow arrived on target too late. Uncle Patrick laughed. "Of course it's all right. We'll be pleased and proud to have ye stayin' with us, won't we, Elsa?"

"Of course," she said, not too convincingly. "I'll go get the coffee."

"I'll help," Trudy said, jumpin' up so fast she almost upset the sauerkraut bowl, which wouldn't in my opinion have been a great loss.

The kitchen was in my line of sight, and I could see Trudy and her mother havin' a heated discussion. Every now and then one of them would gesture toward our table. It didn't take a great deal of imagination to figure out that they were talkin' about us, and they were not happy.

45

7

Uncle Patrick's apartment had five rooms. There was the parlor and the dining room and the kitchen all lined up one behind the other. Then there were two bedrooms, one off the kitchen for Uncle Patrick and Elsa and one off the dining room for the two girls. Friedrich had a small cot by the kitchen stove.

There was more space here than in our whole house in Limerick, which consisted of one room downstairs and a bedroom upstairs with a curtained-off section where Maureen and I slept.

At first Uncle Patrick offered the girls' bedroom to us, but Trudy dragged her mother into the hall, where we could hear her whinin' even with the door closed. Elsa came back and suggested that she and Uncle Patrick would give us their bedroom. By then Ma was gettin' the picture. She said we didn't want to be puttin' anybody out and we'd be just as happy spreadin' our feather bed on the parlor floor.

Well, didn't Trudy and Elsa have to go have another discussion about that. I edged near the hall door to eavesdrop. Now I knew why Da always said ye should mind yer own business, or end up hearin' somethin' ye'd wish ye hadn't.

Elsa's voice was just a low hum, but Trudy's sharp words cut through the door like a spoon through lard. "They've been traveling in steerage for the last two weeks, Mother. Can you imagine what manner of vermin they must be carrying with them? That feather bed should be burned before it unloads its cargo of fleas and lice into our flat. There might even be mice in that filthy thing. And they all need baths."

I heard the murmur of Elsa's voice, then Trudy again. "But, Mother, they're dirty. They smell like goats. I don't think they've ever seen a bar of soap."

I was so angry I wanted to go in that hall and yank Trudy's yellow braid until she squealed like a pig. Dirty indeed! Ma took such good care of that feather bed, it was in perfect condition. She had kept it tied up tight in a linen tablecloth all the way from Ireland, and she had hung it with a bit of string from the bunk above hers, so it couldn't come in contact with the bedding in the ship. She was every bit as worried about the ship's vermin as Trudy was.

As for us needin' baths, Trudy might have a point about that, but it wasn't because we didn't use soap. The only baths we could get on board were with cold seawater. It was possible to get a bath with warm freshwater, but it cost dear, over three times the price of the seawater. No matter how we tried to scrub ourselves with the soap we'd brought along, the saltwater left a scum on our skin that we couldn't rinse off. My hair had become so sticky it was hard to get a brush through it.

I was glad Ma hadn't heard Elsa's remarks, but she soon figured out what was going on when Elsa and Trudy offered to "freshen up" our feather bed, then proceeded to take it out on the fire escape and beat the livin' daylights out of it with brooms for the next half-hour. Ma thanked them when they brought it in, but her face was red. I couldn't tell if it was from anger or embarrassment.

It wasn't until Elsa suggested baths to us that I realized they had an indoor bathroom with a sink, tub, and flushin' terlet. We had heard of these things, but never seen one. Even Grandma Nolan, who was pretty well off by Limerick standards, still used an outdoor privy.

"Here are towels and soap for you," Elsa said.

"We won't be needin' yer soap," I snapped. "We have our own."

Elsa held out a creamy white oval. "I just thought you'd like something special after your long trip. This one's lavender. It always makes me feel wonderful when I use it. Come, let me show you how to work the tap. The faucets here might operate differently from the ones in Ireland." Elsa's words sounded kind, but I could tell that she knew we'd never seen indoor plumbin' in our lives. In Limerick, we thought we were lucky to have a tap right in the yard, instead of havin' to carry water up flights of stairs, the way they did in the tenements.

Wonder of wonders, the one faucet gave out hot water. There was no need to boil water and lug the steamin' pot. And the tub was long enough so a full-grown person could stretch her legs all the way out, instead of havin' her knees bump against her chin the way they did in our washtub at home.

Ma bathed with Bridget first and got her off to bed, then it was Maureen's turn, then mine. "Mind you don't take too long," Ma said. "There's a whole family still needin' to bathe."

The water had cooled, so I added some hot from the faucet and slid down till I was submerged up to my neck. What a glorious feelin' it was. And to think that ordinary people could live like this, not just the rich folks. I lathered up my hair with the fragrant soap, then slid all the way under to rinse it out. The water finally cooled enough to make me shiver, and I didn't dare use up any more of the magic hot water, so I got out, dried off, and cleaned the tub after the water had drained. I wasn't goin' to give Trudy another chance to call us dirty.

When I came out, I was surprised to find that everyone had gone to bed. I could hear some talkin' in the girls' room, but the lights were off. I slid open the door to the parlor and climbed in under the blanket Elsa had given us. Though it was a bit crowded on the feather bed, it was a far sight better than sleepin' on the cots in steerage. The feather bed was still chilled from bein' out on the fire escape, but I moved my feet around until I found a warm spot.

Lyin' in bed, I could hardly list all the events of the day in my mind. I'd started out in the stinkin' bowels of our steamer, heated only by the crush of other human bodies. Now I was curled up in the warm parlor of my uncle's apartment in America with the isinglass windows on the woodstove makin' orange patterns flicker across the ceiling.

Uncle Patrick was warm and welcomin', and reminded me so much of Da in his looks, voice, and the way he flung his hands about when he talked, it made my heart break and swell with joy at the same time. But the rest of the family, at least Elsa and Trudy, weren't as friendly. I could excuse some of it because of the surprise. If someone drops on yer doorstep without so much as a word of warnin', it might take an hour or so to get used to the idea that they're stayin'.

But there was more to it. Except for Uncle Patrick, they all looked on us as foreigners, and dirty ones at that. I should have felt safe here, but I had a strange dread about our stay with our new American family. I hoped Da got back soon.

8

 After complainin' for two weeks about the rollin' and tossin' of the ship, I spent the night thrashin' around for the lack of motion. Ma woke us early. "Let's be up and out of the way before the rest of 'em arise."

"Where will we go?" Maureen asked, rubbin' the sleep from her eyes.

"We'll not go anywhere. I just want to have our things gathered up so they won't be trippin' over us while they get ready to go to Mass."

I had forgotten it was Sunday. Suddenly I looked forward to the comfort of goin' to church in this strange country. When Ma was afraid to be leavin' our parish at home, our priest had told her that the Mass would be the same in America as it was in Limerick, probably one of the few familiar things we'd find here. We dressed and made ourselves ready, but hadn't heard any sounds from the rooms beyond the door, even when we each slipped into the bathroom.

I carefully unpacked my good dress and smoothed out the creases. Ma had made it for me just a few months before we left. In Limerick she was a seamstress for a fancy shop on O'Connell Street, and they had paid her only a small fraction of what they sold the dresses for. The shop owner must have felt guilty about that, because every now and then he'd let Ma have some fabric, usually something that was damaged. The piece she made my dress of was silk taffeta in a new color called "ashes of roses." It had some water stains on it, but Ma cut the pattern so none of them showed. I'd never had anything quite so grand. Though I tried not to be prideful, I couldn't help but notice in the mirror how the soft rose color brought out the blush in my cheeks.

"What time do you think they have Mass here?" Maureen asked. "I'm half starved."

"We'll pick up somethin' to bring home for breakfast after church," Ma said. "They should be comin' out soon."

"I'm goin' outside," I said. The heavy drapes in the parlor covered the windows, and I wanted to see what our new neighborhood looked like.

"Mind ye stay just outside the building," Ma said. "I don't know which Mass we'll be goin' to. It's already too late for eight o'clock."

I knew Ma must be annoyed that Uncle Patrick's family was sleepin' in so late. At home she liked to get to the first Mass so the day wasn't half gone by the time we got home. My dress made a rich rustlin' sound as I ran down the stairs and out into the mornin'. It was cold enough to send my breath steamin' into the air, but the bright sun gave promise of a nice day.

I could see the el at the end of the street, so I started walkin' toward it. The neighborhood was filled with brick and stone buildings packed side by side. Each one was five or six stories in height with a stoop leadin' to the front entrance.

I heard a door open and close, and Maureen came runnin' after me. I didn't stop, but she caught up. "What do ye think?"

"What do I think about what?" I was annoyed that the few minutes I might have had to be alone with my thoughts had ended abruptly.

"You know, the girls. They don't seem too friendly, especially yer friend Trudy."

"Who says she's *my* friend? She hasn't spoken one word to me."

"Well, she's closer to yer age than mine. Hildegarde would be my friend if she weren't so pleased with herself. I can tell she thinks she's better than me." Maureen squinted at me, the sun full in her face. "They are better than us, aren't they? I mean, they have such nice things, they must have a lot of money."

In this light Maureen's eyes looked like pale-blue beach glass, and her black hair gleamed in the sun. She was much prettier than either of the two sour dumplin's upstairs, though I didn't tell her that for fear of makin' her conceited. "Money doesn't make them any better than us. Besides, now that we're in America, we'll be able to earn money and have nice things, too."

"Then we won't have to live with Uncle Patrick anymore, will we? We can leave as soon as Da gets here?"

"Absolutely. But livin' here may not be so bad. Once we all get to know each other, I'm sure things will be fine." I didn't really believe that, but I thought it was best to keep Maureen happy. When she got upset, she often said more than she should, and that could make things even more uncomfortable than they already were. The cold finally found its way through my woolen coat, makin' me shiver. "Let's go inside and find out when we're leavin' for Mass."

As we climbed the stairs, we were met by the smell of fryin' meat. My stomach cramped from hunger. One of the neighbors was havin' a good breakfast. But when we opened the door to the apartment, we saw that it was Elsa who was cookin' sausage, along with a full dozen fried eggs. She seemed to be slammin' the pans and utensils around with more than what I would have considered necessary noise.

"Did everybody go to Mass already?" I asked before I noticed that Ma's face looked like a storm cloud. Somethin' had obviously happened while we were outside.

"Yer father's brother and his family don't go to Mass," Ma said. "They'll be takin' themselves to church. The *Lutheran* church, if ye please." She spat out the word "Lutheran" with so much contempt, ye would have thought Uncle Patrick would be waltzin' his wife and children into a house of ill repute.

In spite of the fact that he was a full ten years older than Ma, Uncle Patrick blushed and shuffled his feet like a scolded schoolboy. "It's not so bad as ye think, Margaret. Ye'll see when ye've been here a while. Some of the old ways . . . Well, things are done different here, is all."

"Old ways?" Ma's eyes were shootin' sparks now. "I'm sure the Holy Mother of God must be pleased to hear that she's nothin' more than the old ways." Ma crossed herself, as if she thought she might have blasphemed even though she was standin' up for the Holy Virgin. Then she turned to us. "You children get it into your heads right now, there'll be no fallin' away from the Church. I don't care if we're the last practicin' Catholics in all of New York. Is that understood?"

"Yes, Ma," Maureen and I mumbled. Bridget looked puzzled, but said nothin'. It must be nice to be so young ye don't understand what's goin' on, I thought. It was bad enough that Uncle Patrick's wife and daughters didn't like us, but the fact that they'd taken him away from the Church was too much to forgive. I knew now that our stay with this family would be more than uncomfortable. What would Da think about this? And how could we possibly live here until he got back?

Ma pulled on her shawl with the flourish of a matador. "Come, children," she said. "We're goin' to Mass."

"Do ye want directions to a Catholic church?" Uncle Patrick asked.

"Not from a heathen," Ma said, and swept us through the door.

9

Ma led us down the sidewalk like a general marchin' the troops off to war. I had to scoop up Bridget in my arms, because she couldn't keep up and Ma seemed to have forgotten about her. It was hard to see, because we were headed into the sun. As bright as it was, I noticed it hadn't done much to warm the air.

"Do ye know where we're goin', Ma?" I asked.

"We're walkin' until we find a church."

"But maybe we're headin' the wrong way. Maybe we should ask someone."

When we passed into the shadow of the Third Avenue el tracks, the cold and dampness settled around us. Ma didn't answer me. She just turned and started walkin' along the sidewalk under the el. Every time a train went overhead, we were sprayed with cinders, and the deafenin' noise set Bridget cryin'. Ma led us to the next street, which was Second

Avenue. I liked the way the streets all had numbers in New York. That would make it easy to find our way around. After a few more blocks, we found a Catholic church. Ma acted as if she'd known all along it would be there.

When we went inside, I felt peace flood over me. This church was larger than St. Mary's in Limerick, but the rosy glow from the stained-glass windows was the same. We genuflected and slipped into a pew. When I knelt and closed my eyes, the smell of incense, the soft click of rosary beads, and the sound of the bells made me feel I was back home. I still had no idea if Da and poor little Joseph had started back to Ireland, or if they were bein' held on Ellis Island. I decided they must be gone, otherwise he would have tried to send word to Uncle Patrick. That was good. The sooner he left, the sooner he'd be back. I realized I hadn't been payin' attention, so I pulled out my rosary beads and joined in the "Hail Mary."

After church, we stopped at a bakery for scones, but found they didn't make them. Instead, Ma bought a flat apple cake with cinnamon and sugar sprinkled over the top.

"May we have some now?" Maureen asked. "I'm about to die of starvation."

"You'll survive until we get home," Ma said. "It wouldn't be polite to eat part of it before we get there."

But when we got home, we found nobody there. Luckily, Uncle Patrick had given Ma an extra key to the apartment, or we would have been stuck outside.

There was a note on the table.

Margaret—

I've left breakfast in the pan for you to heat up. We will be back after church service.

—Elsa

I looked into the pan. The fat from the sausage had congealed over the eggs, makin' the whole mess look like it was encased in wax. My stomach almost turned over. "Let's just eat our cake. This looks terrible."

"We don't waste food," Ma said. "Elsa made this for us, and it would be an insult to her not to eat it."

"Who cares if it's an insult to Elsa?" Maureen said. "She's been insultin' us since we arrived."

"All right, then," Ma said. "Wastin' this food would be an insult to all the poor Irish who starved durin' the famine."

I was goin' to point out that all those people were dead and wouldn't care one way or t'other if we lapped up this greasy mess, but I thought better of it. Ma was in somewhat happier spirits since Mass, and I didn't want to spoil her mood. So we ate the eggs and sausage and saved the cake for the rest of the family. Once Ma heated the pan to melt the grease, it wasn't so bad after all, except that the egg yolks were all hard and I preferred them runny.

Still, I was grateful for a full stomach. This was certainly much better than what passed for food on the ship. When we had boarded, we were each given a cheap tin dish and cup and served ourselves from a huge kettle. Since we washed our own dishes with nothin' but saltwater to do it in, the dishes and cups soon rusted out, givin' a tinny taste to everything we ate or drank. I figured, no matter what we got at Uncle Patrick's, it had to be better than that.

We had just finished our meal and cleared up when the family returned. Though everyone was pretendin' things were fine, there was no doubt that tension hung over us like a swingin' sword.

Ma showed Elsa the cake. "We picked this up for ye. Thought ye might like a bite after church."

"That's very nice, but we'll be having dinner now," Elsa said.

Uncle Patrick stepped in and took the cake from Ma. "Now, isn't that a pretty thing? I think I'll have a piece of that right now. Who'll join me?"

"You'll spoil your appetite for dinner," Elsa said.

Uncle Patrick laughed. "I'll worry about me own appetite, Elsa." He brought plates to the table and started slicin' the cake. Little Friedrich crowded in to get a piece.

"Friedrich," Elsa called from the kitchen. "Come here. You're not allowed to have dessert before your dinner."

Uncle Patrick's face got red, but I noticed he didn't contradict his wife. He only laughed again and said, "That's all the more for us, right?"

Ma, Maureen, Bridget, and I sat with Uncle Patrick while his American family stayed in the kitchen, preparin' dinner. I was already full from the sausages and eggs, but I knew I had to have a piece of cake anyway. A contest was goin' on here, with one team sittin' at the table and the other standin' at the stove. We would vote by eatin' or not eatin' the cake.

Poor Friedrich hung in the doorway, watchin'. I had the urge to call him over like a puppy and slip him a morsel under the table. He was such a quiet child, with sad eyes. I didn't envy him his life, with a harsh mother and two bossy older sisters.

"Did ye find a Catholic church?" Uncle Patrick asked.

"We did," Ma said. I thought this would start up the argument all over again, but Ma appeared to have softened. "I'm afraid I owe you an apology, Patrick. It's none of my business where ye go to church. It just came as a shock to me, is all."

Uncle Patrick patted her hand. "Don't give it another thought, Margaret."

We ate in silence for a few minutes. Then Uncle Patrick started tellin' about how it was when he first came to America, twelve years ago. He began by workin' on the docks. Then he worked his way into politics, as did many Irishmen, apparently. "I'll be able to get a good job for Michael when he arrives," he said. "I may not be very far up in the party yet, but there are those who owe me favors."

I thought at first that Uncle Patrick was tellin' us about himself to help Ma see why he had left the Church, but there wasn't a mention of religion. I noticed he also forgot to mention how he met and married Elsa.

10

Things seemed strained in Uncle Patrick's house over the next week. Ma, Maureen, and I kept tryin' to help Elsa with the household chores, but she always said we were her guests and shouldn't have to work. Even though her words were delivered with a smile, there was somethin' in her manner that made me feel she wanted us to appear lazy. I made a special point of offerin' to help in front of Uncle Patrick so he'd know we were tryin' to do our part around the house.

As for Hildegarde and Trudy, we barely saw them. They left for school first thing in the mornin' and came home just before supper. Neither of them had much to say to Maureen and me, other than askin' us to pass things to them at the table. I once inquired about us goin' to school, too, but Elsa said it wouldn't be a good idea to start in the middle of the school year. Then, later, I found out that both Trudy and

Hildegarde went to a fancy private school for girls over on Fifth Avenue. I couldn't tell whether the girls just didn't want their poor cousins taggin' along or if they thought we'd expect Uncle Patrick to pay our way. Ma told me she was sure there was a public school we could go to, or maybe a school connected to the parish church.

Tuesday night the next week, I was in the bathroom when I overheard a conversation between Uncle Patrick and Elsa. I sat on the rim of the tub and pressed my ear to the wall. I knew it wasn't right to listen, but sometimes a person just needs to know what's goin' on. The head of their bed must have been against the wall, because it was easy to make out what they were sayin'.

"How long do you plan to let this go on, Patrick?"

"What are ye talkin' about?"

"Your relatives. How long do you plan to let them stay?"

"As long as they be needin' a roof over their heads. Ye don't expect me to put them out on the street in the middle of winter, do ye?"

There was a pause here, and I could imagine that Elsa was plannin' another approach. Finally, she spoke. "It's a lovely family, and of course I enjoy having them here, but wouldn't they be happier in a place of their own?"

"And what would they use to pay for that, I ask ye?"

"Didn't Margaret give you some money the first night they arrived? Why don't you give it back to her so they can use it for rent and food for themselves?"

"The money she gave me would barely pay for a few weeks on Broome Street, with not much left over for food. I'm savin' that for Michael. He had planned to get a job as soon as he got here. The money was just enough to hold them over until he got a week's pay."

"But they must be so uncomfortable."

"Have ye heard them complain?"

Elsa cleared her throat or coughed, I couldn't tell which. "They haven't complained in so many words, but I can tell they feel crowded. After all, they have no privacy."

"Well, until they say somethin' to me, they stay right here. This city isn't a good place for a woman to be on her own. If the oldest was a boy, that might help. At least Margaret would have a man to protect her. But not a woman with three girls. They'd be fair game for every con man in New York."

That made me angry. We'd be perfectly able to manage for ourselves. We might be new in the country, but we weren't stupid. The problem was that we had no money to rent a place of our own.

"I wasn't going to mention it," Elsa continued, "but this has created a painful situation for Trudy. She has no place to see Walter. He was courting her in our parlor. Now it's filled with sleeping relatives."

"Well, they have no business courtin' after the family has gone to sleep anyway," Uncle Patrick said. "Let them do their talkin' at Walter's house. It's not far from here, and he can walk her home. Now, that's the end of it."

There was silence after this. Either Elsa had given up, or she knew better than to push Uncle Patrick any further. I wondered how they had come to marry. She seemed so cold, not at all like my other aunts at home. As a matter of fact, the thought that Elsa was my aunt startled me. No one had suggested we call her that, and I knew the name "Aunt Elsa" would stick in my throat if I tried.

So the real reason Trudy didn't like us was that we were crampin' her style with her beau. That was a useful bit of news. It was also good to know that Ma had given Uncle Patrick enough money to pay for a few weeks on a place called Broome Street. Maybe, if I could find a job the way Da had planned to, I could bring in enough money to rent a place on this Broome Street, at least until Da got back. I decided not to mention anything to Ma. I didn't want her to know that Elsa was tryin' to get rid of us, although she had probably figured that out on her own. But if I could find some work, we could leave here with our dignity intact. I decided to look for a job first thing in the mornin'.

Wednesday, at breakfast, I made a point of eatin' very little. I didn't want Elsa complainin' about how much it cost to feed us. When I had earned a day's pay, we wouldn't have to rely on charity anymore. Ma raised her eyebrows in a question when she saw how little I had taken on my plate. I just shrugged and smiled. Then, as soon as the girls left for school and Uncle Patrick went to work, I pulled my coat around me.

Ma was sittin' in the parlor with Bridget on her lap. "Where are ye goin', Margaret Rose?"

"It's Rose," I said.

Ma rolled her eyes. "All right. Where are ye goin', *Rose*. And I'm only callin' ye that because it's yer legal American name and I don't want to break the law."

I looked to make sure Elsa was out of earshot, then told Ma about my plan to find work so we could move out.

"Oh, I don't know. Yer father said we should stay here until he got back."

"But, Ma, even if they sent him and Joseph back right away, they wouldn't reach Ireland until Saturday. Then he has to work at least a month to earn his passage, and it will take another two weeks for the ship to get him back here."

Maureen was countin' on her fingers. "That's over six weeks. It'll be the middle of April before he gets back. I'll never last that long without gettin' into a fight with Trudy or Hildegarde."

Tears came to Ma's eyes. "Six weeks? I miss yer father so much. And poor Joseph. How I long to see my baby."

When she started to cry, Bridget turned in Ma's lap and patted her cheek. "Don't be sad, Ma. Da and Joseph will come soon."

This only made Ma cry harder. I was gettin' worried about Ma. At home she was always so sure of herself, but here she seemed afraid. She'd hardly left the house except for when we went to Mass. That's why I was surprised when she wiped her eyes and said, "It should be me gettin' the job. You can stay here and take care of Bridget and Maureen."

"No, Ma. Let me try to find work first. I don't want to be left alone with Elsa. I'll lose my temper for sure and get us all into trouble."

Elsa came into the room and discovered us whisperin' together. "Is something wrong?"

"Everything's fine," I said, smilin' sweetly and lyin' through my teeth.

11

I couldn't believe Ma had agreed to let me go out and look for work, but then it occurred to me that she didn't think I'd find anything. If I came back without a job, then she could have me stay home tomorrow watchin' the children, and she'd go find a position as a seamstress. It was certain that Ma had more skills than me, but that didn't necessarily mean she'd make more money as a seamstress than I would as a . . . I couldn't finish that thought, because I hadn't any idea what kind of work I might find.

I decided to head in the same direction we had gone to church, drawn by the fact that it had felt familiar, and maybe hopin' that there would be a shop nearby that would remind me of Limerick, too. But this time I crossed over to Second Avenue right away. I stopped in a small shoe shop on the corner of Tenth Street. I was bein' very careful to notice the streets so I could find my way home later. The cobbler looked up when I came in, but didn't say anything and went back to his work. I suppose he could tell I wasn't rich enough to buy a pair of shoes.

I cleared my throat, but he ignored me. "Excuse me, sir. I was wonderin' if ye might have some work I could do."

The man raised his eyebrows. "Work? Do you know how to cut leather?"

"No, but I . . ."

He interrupted me with rapid-fire questions. "Can you put in eyelets? Nail a sole? Place a heel?"

"I'm a fast learner," I said. "Ye'd only need to show me once."

He stood and came over to the counter. "Learn this, then, fast learner. It took me five years as an apprentice to learn this skill. There's a boatload of you greenhorns landing every day, and you all think you're going to make a fortune in America. Well, don't hold your breath, girlie, because it's not going to happen." Then he laughed, showin' a mouthful of crooked yellow teeth.

I ran from the shop and kept runnin', tears stingin' my eyes. So Elsa and her daughters weren't the only ones who wouldn't welcome us with open arms. They even had a name for newcomers here—"greenhorns."

I finally stopped and leaned against a lamppost to catch my breath. I wouldn't let one nasty man keep me from gettin' a job. Maybe makin' shoes was too hard a job to start with. I needed somethin' simple, like being a shop girl. I could help people find what they were lookin' for. It might even be fun.

When I looked up at the street sign, I realized I had gotten myself turned around and had run along Tenth Street. But as long as the streets were numbered, I couldn't get lost.

I stopped in several more shops—all small family stores, each run by a shopkeeper and his wife, and they couldn't afford to hire an extra worker. Then I saw the biggest store I had ever laid eyes on. It took up the entire block. Surely it would take dozens of shop girls to make this store run.

I went through the front entrance and walked around the ground floor, lookin' over the cases filled with purses, gloves, and scarves. There were both men and women workin' here. The women dressed in the same white bodice favored by Hildegarde and Trudy, with sleeves that pouffed out at the shoulder, then fit tight from elbow to wrist. There were lots of little tucks in the bodice that made the waist small, and a collar snug around the neck. It seemed since Mr. Gibson had painted his famous beauty, every girl in New York wanted to look exactly like her. I couldn't help but think how I might look in a blouse like that, with my hair fluffed up and knotted on top in the Gibson Girl style. As soon as I had a job, I'd use some of the money to get a nice shirtwaist.

I climbed the grand staircase to where I could look over the railing and see most of the ground floor. Ladies in fine coats and hats moved through the rows of tables and counters, some accompanied by their maids. On the next floor, there was an elegant salon where ladies could find dresses and gowns. A lovely woman about Ma's age was showin' a black satin gown with bugle beads to a wealthy-lookin' woman. I could just imagine the feel of that slippery satin. I watched the woman wave away the black dress. As the saleswoman started off to find another selection, she noticed me. "I don't think you'll find anything suitable for yourself here," she said.

"Oh, I'm not lookin' for a dress, ma'am, but I'd like to work here, doin' just what you do."

The saleswoman lifted her chin. "Well, since I'm doing what I do, there's really no need for you to be doing what I do, now, is there?"

She looked with disdain at my homespun dress, even though it was clean and freshly ironed. I wished she could see the dresses my mother made for the fancy dress shop in Limerick. They were every bit as beautiful as the garments here. It seemed to me that the person who could make a fine dress was just as good if not better than the person who merely sold it. After all, if the dress was poorly made, the saleswoman would be hard-pressed to convince anyone to buy it.

I ran back to the ground floor and out the door. I wouldn't want to work in such a snooty place anyway.

I was almost ready to give up when I noticed the lovely fragrance of bakin' bread. It reminded me of the bread Ma baked at home. I followed my nose to a small shop. Now I was on a street called Bowery. What happened to the numbers? I decided not to worry about directions and went inside. Workin' in a place that smelled like this would be heaven.

There was a pleasant woman behind the counter. "What can I be gettin' for ye?" she asked in an Irish accent that sounded so much like my Aunt Mary Clare, I almost burst into tears from joy.

"I'm lookin' for work," I said. "Do ye have somethin' I could do? I'm a hard worker."

The woman smiled. "Ah, it's from Limerick ye've come? And not long ago, either, is it? Ye're a greenhorn?"

The word comin' from her lips didn't seem a criticism.

"Yes, we've just arrived, only the week before last. Are ye from Limerick, too?"

The woman shook her head. "I'm from Cork, and it's been a good many years since I've seen the old sod, but I can still tell where an Irish person comes from, even if they've been here for a while."

"So do ye think ye might have work for me?" I asked, trying to get her back on the subject.

"I'm sorry, dear. My husband does the bakin' and I do the sellin'. We only take in enough to support the two of us."

She must have seen the disappointment on my face, because she wiped her hands on her apron and wrote somethin' on a piece of paper for me.

"Go to this man and tell 'im that Colleen Murphy sent ye."

"What kind of place is this?" I asked.

"He runs a shop that makes paper flowers. My niece worked for 'im for a while. When she learned how to do it, he let her take the work home so her mother and sisters could do it, too. He's not Irish, but he was fair with the money."

"Oh, thank ye," I said. I started to leave, but Mrs. Murphy called me back. She wrapped a muffin in paper and handed it to me. "It's a long walk, dear. Ye'll be needin' this for lunch." Then she took me out on the sidewalk and pointed in the direction I should go. "Follow the Bowery all the way to Hester Street. His shop is on Chrystie Street, one block over. It's in the back."

I thanked her again and was on my way. This could be the answer to our problems. If I could get work to bring back to Ma and even Maureen, we could earn money three times as fast as one person workin' alone. My feet fairly flew over the sidewalks as I rushed to find the address written on the slip of paper. It was easy until I reached Houston Street. There the numbers stopped and the streets all had names instead. I tried to memorize the streets as I passed them—Stanton, Rivington, Delancey, Broome. Broome! So this was the place we could afford to live? It was crowded and run-down, with a mixture of old brick buildings and wooden ones. Most of the people in the street looked strange to me, with odd clothing. Still, I'd sooner live on the outskirts of hell than with Elsa and her girls.

I kept goin' until I found Hester Street. It was jammed with people sellin' everything from fruit to underdrawers from pushcarts. I'd never seen so many people in one place. There were awnings hangin' out into the street, and horse-drawn carriages tryin' to make their way through the mess.

I went one block over to Chrystie Street, and finally I found number twenty-eight, Mr. Moscovitz's building. It had no sign showin' there was a business inside. Nobody came to answer when I knocked. I began to feel afraid. What if Mr. Moscovitz turned out to be as mean as the man in the shoe shop? Then I decided if he could give me a job I could put up with any harsh words he could speak.

I took a deep breath and turned the doorknob. It was unlocked. I looked again on the slip of paper and saw that there was an apartment number listed—number four. I moved through the dark hall, watchin' to make sure nobody jumped out at me from the shadows. Mean words were hurtful, but there were worse things that could happen to a girl. I wished I had brought one of Ma's long hairpins with me to protect myself. I had the feelin' Ma would be none too pleased if she could see where I was now.

I got to the end of the hall and found apartment number three. But Mrs. Murphy had said it was in the back. I noticed in the shadows that there was a door with no number at the end of the hall. I knocked, and when nobody answered, I opened it. Bright sunlight and a blast of cold air hit me. It was the end of the building, but there was a smaller building behind it. And I could see that the sign on the front door said four. When I knocked on that door, a man's voice said, "Come in."

I found a room crammed with two long tables, a group of women and young girls sittin' around each one. The tables were heaped with piles of flower parts—stems, leaves, and bright paper petals. Bunches of paper roses hung from a wire. The room hummed with low conversation, none of it in a language I could understand.

A man stepped out of the back corner by the woodstove. "What do you want?"

I went over and handed him the slip of paper. "Colleen Murphy said ye might have work for me."

He looked at the paper and handed it back to me. I realized it only had his name and address, no proof that it came from her. "And how do you know Mrs. Murphy?"

"We're both from Ireland." I knew this didn't answer his question, but it wasn't a lie. I thought he might not want to hire me if he knew I'd just met her today, and only for a few minutes at that.

The man smiled. "Ireland, eh? I'd never have guessed."

There was some quiet tittering from the two tables. I heard a nearby girl say to another, "Greenie," and they laughed again.

Could everyone in New York tell that I had just stepped off the boat from Ireland? And why was that something to be ashamed of?

Mr. Moscovitz looked me over from head to toe. "So—you know how to make paper roses?"

I glanced quickly at the table. It didn't seem too hard. I could simply follow what the person next to me was doin'. I had learned from the shoemaker that it didn't pay to tell someone ye could learn fast. If ye wanted a job, ye had to know how to do it. I couldn't make myself come right out and say yes, so I only nodded. I had the feelin' I'd still have to mention this at confession Saturday night. A lie is a lie, whether you speak it or not.

Mr. Moscovitz rocked back on his heels. "An experienced

rose-maker. This is my lucky day. What's your name, girl?"

"Rose," I said.

Mr. Moscovitz turned toward the girls. He was obviously playin' to them now. "A rose-maker named Rose."

There were many comments flyin' around the room. I couldn't make out the words, but I knew their intent was to mock me. I bit my tongue to keep from cryin'. I came here to make money, not friends, but I missed my chums from home. I had always been popular, and now I was the outsider. I didn't like the way it felt.

Mr. Moscovitz pulled out a chair, made a big show of dustin' it off with his handkerchief. "Come, Miss Rose the rose-maker. I give you the best job in the shop. You're a peddler, no?"

I didn't know what to say. First he was talkin' about makin' roses and now he wanted me to sell them? Would I have to push a cart through the streets? Then Mr. Moscovitz put a wired stem with leaves and a pile of red petals in front of me, and I realized he meant for me to be a "petaler," not a peddler. I was glad I hadn't opened my mouth and made a fool of myself.

Mr. Moscovitz stood watchin' over me, his arms folded and his toe tappin' impatiently.

The girls were silent now, but two dozen pairs of dark eyes watched me from under thick lashes. I wanted to run away, but I couldn't pass up a job. I was the only blue-eyed person in the room, the only greenie, and the only one who had not an idea in the world how to make roses.

12

I picked up a stem and stole a quick glance at the girl next to me. As she twirled the stem she kept pickin' up petals, which seemed to attach themselves magically, one after another, until she had a perfect rose in full bloom. She daintily dropped her rose into a pile and started on the next.

I fingered the pile of petals, tryin' to get hold of a single piece, but my hands were sweaty, stickin' several petals together. The dye made the tips of my fingers look blood-stained. I dropped the ruined petals and wiped my hand on my skirt. I could hear giggles all around me. I started again. By this time the girl next to me had finished her second rose and started a third.

I wrapped a petal around the stem, then grabbed another. When I had six petals clumped on the end of the stem, I noticed that the girl next to me was twistin' a thin wire over every petal as she put it on. I reached for the wire, but I was too late. All of my petals fell in a heap. There was the burst of laughter I had learned to expect. Mr. Moscovitz shushed the girls and I tried again. I managed to wire nine petals to the stem, but the end result was all misshapen.

Mr. Moscovitz took it from me and held it up. "Girls, girls, look what we have here. It's a Wild Irish Rose."

This time the laughter sounded like an explosion.

"I'm glad I can be such greenie entertainment for ye," I said. "If someone will show me how to do this, I can learn."

"But you said you knew how." Mr. Moscovitz's voice was all sweet and oily. "You lied to me?"

"I didn't think ye'd give me a job if I said I didn't know how to do it."

He shook his head. "Not necessarily. I can always use a worker who's willing to learn."

I pushed back my chair. "Then I was wrong to lie. I'm sorry I wasted yer time."

He let me get as far as the door, then said, "Make room for Rose at the end of the stem table. That *is* your name, isn't it? You didn't lie about that?"

"Yes, Rose is my real name."

Mr. Moscovitz pretended to wipe his forehead. "Such a relief. Otherwise we'd have to call you Peony when we make peonies and Sweet Pea when we make sweet peas."

This time I laughed with the rest of the girls. How silly I must have looked, comin' in pretendin' I was a rose-maker. Mr. Moscovitz seemed genuinely fond of the girls in his shop. Maybe he made jokes just to pass the time. After all, it must get tedious doin' the same thing over and over.

A pretty young girl got up from the end of the other table, moved her chair, and dragged another one over next to it.

"Thank you, Tessa," Mr. Moscovitz said. "You can show Rose the first step of making the stems."

Tessa smiled at me. "It's not hard. You just take a piece of wire and twist the paper around it like this." She held the roll of green paper in her left hand and spun the wire in the fingers of her right hand. The paper strip spiraled evenly down the wire, and she ripped it off at the end.

My first attempt was clumsy, but Tessa adjusted the position of the strip for me, and soon I was pickin' up speed.

Mr. Moscovitz came around the table and put his hand on my shoulder. "That's better, Rose. You'll work your way up to petaler yet." He gave my shoulder a squeeze as he moved on.

"You mustn't let him do that," Tessa whispered when he was out of earshot.

"Do what?" I asked.

"You mustn't let him touch you."

"He didn't hurt me."

Tessa leaned closer, pretendin' to help me with my stem. "Listen, every girl in this room was once a greenhorn like you. Most of us didn't speak English when we arrived, and some of them still don't. But there's one sentence every girl learned to speak before anything else."

"What's that?"

"'Keep your hands to yourself, please.'"

I stifled a laugh.

Tessa shot me a sharp look. "I'm serious, Rose. Mr. Moscovitz was testing you to see how far he could go."

I watched him as he moved around the room. He was older than Da and looked harmless, but I'd keep Tessa's words in mind.

We worked in silence for the next hour. My hands were beginnin' to stiffen up from the cold when Mr. Moscovitz said it was time for lunch. Tessa showed me where the outside privy was. It was vile-smellin', but I needed to use it anyway. The sooner I learned to make roses well enough to take work home, the better off I'd be.

When we went back in, the girls had all gathered around the stove. Tessa poured a cup of hot water from the kettle that had been sittin' on the heat all mornin'. "We all bring cups from home. I'll share mine if you'd like."

I offered her part of my muffin, and we ended up sharin' her black bread and cheese, too. We sat on a pile of cartons in the corner and talked while we ate. I learned that her last name was Carlisi, and she and her family came over from Italy less than a year ago.

"How did ye learn English so quickly?" I asked.

"We learned before we came. My father was a professor at the university. He thought it was important to know other languages. That's why I can understand what the other girls are saying here. Most of the Jewish girls are from

Russia or Poland, so they speak either their native language or Yiddish or a combination."

"Where does yer father teach here in America?" I thought it odd that the daughter of such a learned man would be workin' in a shop like this.

"He doesn't teach." Tessa rolled her eyes. "Here he sweeps up scraps in a clothing factory. He is skilled with books but not with his hands. He would have been better off with a trade."

"But why?"

Tessa shrugged. "Because Italians are not respected here. But it will change. They say there was a time when everyone looked down on the Irish. Now they run the whole city."

I wanted to ask more, but Mr. Moscovitz called everyone back to work. My hands had already learned how to make stems without my mind havin' to help them, so I could concentrate on what was goin' on around me. I could hear the differences in the languages being spoken and saw that the girls had divided themselves into groups from their own countries. I thought it odd, but, then, if another Irish girl walked into the room at that moment, I knew I'd greet her like a long-lost sister.

What Tessa said puzzled me, though. If the Irish ran the city, why did people treat me with so little respect when they found out I was from Ireland?

The afternoon went much more slowly than the mornin'. My neck began to ache, and the seat of the chair felt hard. Once I stood up, and everybody looked at me as if I had committed a crime. I quickly stretched my back and sat down again. I thought I had been workin' quickly, but was surprised to see that my pile of stems wasn't even half as large as Tessa's.

The next time I looked up from my work, I could see through the one tiny window that it was gettin' dark. "What time do we stop workin'?" I whispered to Tessa.

"We finish at eight o'clock."

"I can't stay that long today," I said.

"You didn't even get here until ten o'clock. That's three hours after the rest of us started. You'll be paid little for the day if you leave early."

Mr. Moscovitz must have heard that, because he came over to us. "Is there a problem, Rose the rose-maker?"

It was an old joke now, and nobody bothered to laugh at it. Besides, I seemed to be more accepted by the others since Tessa had taken me under her wing.

"I have to leave, Mr. Moscovitz. My mother will worry if I'm not home for dinner."

Mr. Moscovitz rubbed his beard. "I see. And will she expect you home for dinner every night?"

"I think it will be all right if she knows where I am."

"You *think* it will be all right."

"It will be fine," I mumbled, wonderin' how on earth I could convince Ma to let me come back to this place.

13

Everything looked so different when I got outside. The pushcart peddlers had gone home, leavin' the street more open. I had a false start, headin' in the wrong direction on the Bowery until I got my bearings. Finally, I was passin' the streets with familiar names again, but I didn't feel safe. I didn't know how late it was, but everything was in total darkness except for the pools of light under the street lamps. Every now and then I thought I saw a shadowy figure in a doorway, which set me off runnin'. Finally, I crossed Houston and was on Second Avenue again. I ran most of the twelve blocks back to Uncle Patrick's, slowin' down only to catch my breath. It was freezin' cold, and I almost slipped on a patch of ice at one of the corners. At last, I arrived at the apartment and took the stairs three at a time.

When I went in, everyone but Uncle Patrick was sittin' at

the table havin' dinner. Ma and Elsa shoved back their chairs at the same time and came toward me.

"Where have you been?" Elsa shouted. "We've all been frantic. We thought something terrible had happened to you. Your mother says you went out to find work? Why would you do such a foolish thing when you don't know anything about the city? Why didn't you ask my advice?"

I turned to Ma. She looked stricken. "It's not Rose's fault. I gave her my permission to go."

"What kind of work could a child find?" Elsa shrieked. "Especially a girl. You have no sense, Margaret. No sense at all."

"I have enough sense to know my own child. She has a good head on her shoulders."

Trudy had been watchin' this whole scene with a smug little smile on her face. "Where could you possibly find work? Was it a sweatshop?"

"No," I said. "It's a place where they make flowers."

Elsa's eyes narrowed. "Where is it?"

"Not far."

Trudy echoed her mother. "Where is it?"

"Chrystie Street."

Trudy grabbed her mother's arm. "I knew it! She was working at a filthy sweatshop!"

Elsa looked at me with contempt. "This is unacceptable. Patrick will be terribly upset when he hears about this. As councilman of the Seventeenth Ward, he has a reputation to uphold."

"How does my makin' flowers damage his reputation?"

"Don't you be smart with me, young lady. You must promise me you won't work there anymore. I can't imagine why you would do such a thing."

I wanted to shout, "We need the money so we can get away from you and yer dreadful daughters," but I held back. I knew that Uncle Patrick had been a great help to Ma and Da back in Ireland. He had given them money and a place to stay when they were first married. I didn't want to do anything to hurt him, even though I despised his family.

Elsa was still rantin'. "Patrick will put an end to this when he gets home. If Rose's father is not here, then Patrick will decide what's best for her."

"With her father not here, *I* will make the decisions," Ma said.

Now Ma and Elsa were goin' at it head to head. This wasn't about me anymore. I figured for Ma it had more to do with Elsa takin' Uncle Patrick away from the family and the Catholic Church.

Maureen was standin' behind Elsa and Trudy. She had one hand on her hip, makin' stabbin' motions in the air with the pointer finger of her other hand—a perfect imitation of Elsa.

"You're ignorant about America," Elsa shouted at Ma. "The neighborhood Rose was in isn't safe, *especially* after dark. The pittance she might earn there isn't worth the risk."

"All right," Ma conceded at last. "If the place isn't safe, then she won't go back."

"But, Ma . . ."

"That's the end of it," Ma said. "Elsa knows this city. We don't." Ma had given in, but the look on her face made me think she was still stingin' over Elsa's use of the word "ignorant."

"All right, then." Elsa pulled out her chair and sat down. "Our meal is getting cold. Sit. Eat."

As hungry as I was, I couldn't swallow a bite. Our situation had become intolerable. We couldn't possibly stay here until Da got back. But how could we get out of here if I wasn't allowed to earn some money? I was startled to realize that I had never asked how much I would be paid for my work. All I knew was that Mrs. Murphy said Moscovitz was fair with the money.

Nobody said much after dinner—or durin' the meal, for that matter. When the weight of the silence hangin' over me became too heavy to bear, I put my coat around my shoulders and opened the window to the fire escape.

"Where do you think you're going?" Hildegarde asked.

"Where d'ye think I'm goin'? I'm runnin' off to work in a sweatshop all night."

Hildegarde's eyes widened. "I'm going to tell my mother."

"I was just makin' a joke, ye little dimwit. I only want a breath of fresh air."

As I pulled the window closed behind me, I heard Hildegarde's whiny voice, "Mo-ther! Rose called me a bad name!"

I had barely sat myself down on the fire-escape step when Elsa stuck her head out of the window, chastised me, and made me apologize to her weaselly daughter. It was bad enough puttin' up with the reprimands from my own mother, but havin' Elsa after me was almost more than I could bear. And I didn't remember askin' for two more sisters, unpleasant ones at that. There was only so much a person could take.

After the window closed, I put my head in my hands for a bit of peace, but I heard it open again. It was Maureen this time. She fit herself on the step beside me. "Was it fun?"

"The job? No. It was mostly dull."

"Was it scary?"

"No."

"Did they pay ye a lot of money?"

"No, they pay at the end of the week."

"Are ye goin' back?"

"I don't know."

Maureen stood up and looked over the railing. "Why do they have this little balcony and stairs? Nobody ever goes in or out this way."

"It's just used if there's a fire," I said. "If ye can't get down the stairs, ye go out this way."

"The ladder doesn't even go all the way to the ground. How could ye get the rest of the way down?"

"I don't know," I said, tiring of her questions. "Ye jump the rest of the way, I guess."

Maureen pulled back from the railing. "I could never jump. I wouldn't have the courage."

"Ye'd be amazed how much courage you'd have with flames lickin' at yer arse."

Just then, the window opened and Trudy stuck her head out. "What now?" I asked.

"I just want to tell you that you're a fool. We're gracious enough to take you into our home and you act like a common little harlot, running all over the city at night."

"If ye'll notice, I'm not runnin'. I'm sittin'."

Trudy's eyes narrowed. "You know full well what I'm talking about. It's humiliating that someone in my own family worked in a sweatshop. I'm ashamed to claim you as my cousin."

"Look," I said, standin' up. "As far as I'm concerned, we are no relation to each other at all. My uncle just happened to marry yer mother, is all. A poor decision on his part, I might add."

"You're despicable!" Trudy said, and she slammed the window shut.

"What does that mean?" Maureen asked.

"I don't know. But I have the feelin' it wasn't a compliment."

I had another feelin'—that every time I had words with Elsa or one of her daughters I was turnin' more and more into the person they thought I was.

14

🌹 *That night,* after Elsa and the girls went to bed, Ma and I had a quiet argument. There was no way I could convince her that I should go back to work makin' paper flowers.

"Just listen, Ma," I whispered. "The lady in the bakery said Mr. Moscovitz sometimes lets girls take work home. If I could teach you and Maureen to make stems, then we could make three times the money."

"Where would we do the work, Rose? Elsa would have a fit if we did it here. Ye know how fussy she is about her house. As hard as I try to keep our goods in a neat little pile durin' the day, she's always pokin' at it, tryin' to make it smaller."

"It's only wires and paper strips, Ma. It wouldn't take up any space at all. We could do the work while everybody is away durin' the day and have it cleared up long before they came home."

"But ye'd have to go to that terrible neighborhood to get the work and take back the finished pieces."

"It's not such a bad place, and Elsa just said it wasn't safe at night. It's fine in the daytime. I could go first thing in the mornin'." I held my breath, hopin' Ma wouldn't remember that Elsa had said the neighborhood wasn't safe, *especially* after dark. Then I jumped in with my best argument. "Ye know we can't stay here, Ma. Elsa and her daughters don't like us. They think we're ignorant." I saw her jaw tighten when I said that word, and I knew I had her.

"All right," she said finally. "Ye'll go in the mornin', after everybody has left. But if the man won't let ye bring the work home, ye're to come back right away. Is that understood?"

"Yes, Ma."

Elsa took so long gettin' ready to go out Thursday mornin', I despaired of her leavin' at all. "Where does she go?" I whispered to Ma. "Does she have some sort of job?"

"She goes callin' on people," Ma said. "It has somethin' to do with Patrick bein' a ward councilman. Elsa went on and on about it yesterday, tryin' to let me know how important they both are, I guess."

"Who does she call on?"

Ma shrugged. "Mostly sick people or widows. She says

it's important that people know that the party cares about their hardships."

"I don't think Elsa cares about anybody but herself."

Ma poked me to shut me up just as Elsa came into the room, buttonin' up her coat. It was a beautiful dark-green wool with a fur collar and cuffs. Her hat was a matchin' green with fur trim. How I'd love to see Ma in an outfit like that. Soon as we got on our feet in America, I'd see that she got one. She deserved nice things every bit as much as Elsa—probably more.

"I won't be gone long today," Elsa said, wigglin' her fingers into her kid gloves. "Help yourselves to sauerkraut for lunch."

My stomach lurched at the thought of eatin' sauerkraut, but Ma thanked her as if she had offered us a banquet.

It took Elsa forever to leave. I knew she was watchin' me, so I pretended to be settled in for the day, mendin' my stockings. Finally, she bundled Friedrich in his coat and headed for the door. "I won't be long," she said again, givin' me a stern look to make sure I caught her meaning. After we listened to their footsteps go all the way down the stairs and heard the door slam, I peeked through a slit in the drapes to see which way they were goin'. Elsa turned several times to look back at our building, then disappeared from sight.

All the way over to the shop, I tried to think of a way to convince Mr. Moscovitz to let me take work home. I didn't think there was much of a chance he'd let me do it, but I had to try. At least it was easier to find my way this time, now that I knew where I was goin'. I arrived at the shop just in time to hear the nearby church chimes toll eleven o'clock. I made my way through the front building and waited outside the door of the back tenement. I stayed there partly because I was hopin' that Tessa would come out and give me some advice on what to say, and partly because I was afraid to go in at all.

I finally got up the courage to open the door. Mr. Moscovitz looked up. "Yesterday you leave early and today you arrive late? You shouldn't have bothered to come at all. You're fired."

"Could I just talk with ye for a minute, Mr. Moscovitz?" I asked.

"Why should I talk with a person who doesn't work here?"

"Please, sir?"

"All right. Girls, it's time for lunch."

Tessa gave me a funny look as she left the room. I hoped I'd get a chance to talk to her outside. I explained to Mr. Moscovitz about not bein' able to work here but wantin' to take the work home.

"Why should I trust you to take materials away from here when I couldn't even trust you to come back on time the second day?"

"Please, Mr. Moscovitz, I really need the work. We can't stay where we're livin' now. The three of us need to earn money for rent so we can get our own flat."

"You say three of you can work from home?" He looked interested.

"Yes, sir. Me, my mother, and my sister. I can teach them both how to do stems."

Mr. Moscovitz rubbed his beard. "Of course, I couldn't pay you as much as I would if you were a regular worker here."

"All right." Since I never found out how much I would be earnin' in the first place, I wouldn't know the difference.

"And I'll only pay for perfect stems. The cost of materials for bad stems will come out of your pay."

"Yes, sir. I understand." I was also beginnin' to understand that Mr. Moscovitz would try to pay us as little as possible, but what choice did we have? "What do I get paid for the work I did yesterday?" I asked.

"You ruined so many materials yesterday, you should owe me money. But out of the goodness of my heart, I'm going to call it even." He pinched my cheek. I knew I should tell him to keep his hands off, but I didn't want him to send me away without work.

Mr. Moscovitz went over to the supply table in the corner. "I'm wrapping up enough materials for three thousand stems. Bring them back tomorrow and I'll give you more. I'll keep track of how many perfect stems you make, and you'll get paid on Saturday."

"Three thousand stems in one day?"

"Most of my girls do almost three thousand a day by themselves. You have two other people helping you. I should be able to give you at least five thousand a day by next week."

I took the package from him. "All right. Thank you, Mr. Moscovitz. Ye won't regret this."

"That remains to be seen. I'll tell you this. If you run off with my supplies and don't return with stems, you will have much to regret."

I made a hasty retreat out the door. I saw Tessa talkin' to some other girls in the yard and ran over to her. She looked at the bundle in my arms. "So you're taking home piecework?"

"Yes. This way my mother and sister can work with me. My family won't let me work here all day."

Tessa's dark eyes looked me square in the face. "Why not? You too good for us? They won't let you work in such a dangerous neighborhood?"

I could feel my face gettin' red. "No, it's not that. It's just that . . ."

One of the other girls said somethin' to Tessa in Yiddish, and she laughed. An older woman walked by me and spat on the ground near my feet.

"Why is everybody upset with me? I need to earn money for my family."

"You're taking the work away from us," Tessa said. "Moscovitz will only pay you half as much as he pays us, maybe even less. He'll give you more and more work, because you work so cheap. And when the orders for paper flowers are filled, he'll fire us all and close the shop for the season. Having the three of you work at home will only make that happen faster."

"But I didn't know. . . ."

Tessa turned as she went in the door. "You don't know anything, greenie. I'm sorry I helped you yesterday."

After all the workers had disappeared back into the building, I stood there, stunned. I had no idea that takin' work home would mean the girls in the shop got less work, although it made sense. I felt terrible thinkin' of Tessa's words. "You too good for us? They won't let you work in such a dangerous neighborhood?" I had denied it, but of course that was the truth.

My family wouldn't let me work in this place because they feared for my safety, yet these girls came here every day and left long after dark. Wasn't there someone at home who feared for them?

15

I ran most of the way home. Now that I knew the way, I didn't waste precious time gettin' lost. Ma must have been watchin' for me, because she opened the door before I could reach for the knob. "Did ye enjoy yer walk?" She rolled her eyes toward the kitchen, took the package from my hands, and slipped it under her sweater.

"It was a fine walk," I said. "The fresh air did me a world of good."

Hearin' my voice, Elsa rushed in from the kitchen, wipin' her hands on her apron. "Where did you walk?" she asked, eyein' me suspiciously.

"I don't know. Just around the neighborhood."

Elsa folded her arms. "I was walking around the neighborhood and didn't see any sign of you."

"Leave the girl be, Elsa," Ma said. "I told ye she just wanted to get some fresh air. There's no harm in it."

I took off my coat and went to sit near the fire, smilin' my most innocent smile at Elsa. The rest of the day passed without incident. Hildegarde was snoopin' around me after she got home from school, tryin' to find out where I had been, but when I just smiled and played dumb, she soon lost interest.

By Friday mornin', the subject of my mysterious walk had been forgotten. Elsa and Friedrich had to leave the house early, because the girls wanted them to attend a special event at school. Of course there was no mention of us goin' along, which was fine with me. I could hardly wait to get started on our project.

As soon as Uncle Patrick left the house, I took out the supplies and spread them on the table. Without waitin' for instructions, Maureen grabbed at the bundle of wires, which took on a life of their own and sprang from the table to scatter all over the floor.

"Now look at the mess ye've made," I cried. "Couldn't ye wait to find out what to do?"

"I barely touched them," Maureen protested. "Stop bein' so bossy, Rose."

"Stop yer arguin'," Ma said. "Let's pick these wires up so we can get started."

We spent the next twenty minutes on our hands and knees collectin' the wires. Bridget tried to help, but couldn't pick them up in her pudgy little hands without bendin' them into hairpins. A few wires had lodged in the crevices between the floorboards, makin' them almost impossible to retrieve.

"Can't we just forget the ones in the cracks?" Maureen asked. "Nobody will miss one or two little wires."

"I'm sure that Mr. Moscovitz knew exactly how many wires he gave me. If any of them are missin', he'll subtract some of my pay."

"He doesn't sound like a very nice person," Maureen said.

I was losin' patience with her. "He's not supposed to be nice. He's my boss!" I liked the way that sounded. I'd never had a real job before.

We finally had all our supplies lined up again, and I began the instructions. I thought Maureen would be the hard one to teach, but Ma turned out to be more of a problem. She learned quickly, but then got bored with makin' each stem exactly the same. Instead of rippin' the paper tape off at the end of the wire, she wound it back down the wire about an inch and pinched it into a leaf shape before tearin' it off.

"Ma!" I said. "What are ye doin'?"

Ma twirled the stem, admirin' it. "This is nicer, don't ye think?"

Bridget clapped her hands. "Pretty!" she squealed.

"But, Ma, it's not the way we're supposed to do it."

"Nonsense," Ma said. "I can't imagine that yer Mr. Moscovitz wouldn't rather have a stem with a leaf on it. Maybe several leaves. I'm surprised nobody thought of it before."

"They did think of it, Ma, but that's a whole different job. They have little paper leaves that somebody else puts on the stems after our part is done."

"Why can't we be the ones to do that?" Maureen chimed in. "That would be more fun."

"I'm sure it would," I said. "But we're not after havin' fun here. This is a job that we're gettin' paid for, if the two of ye will just stop complainin'."

I heard Maureen gasp, and I realized I was about to take a tongue-lashin' from Ma. Nobody talked to her like that, not even Da. I was afraid to look up, but when I did, I saw her rollin' up a plain wire just the way she was supposed to. She didn't look pleased about it, though.

Ma caught me lookin' at her. "What?"

I shrugged. "Nothin'. I'm sorry the job is so dull."

"We're gettin' paid for it. That's all that matters."

It wasn't long before we got into the rhythm of the task. And when Bridget drifted off to sleep, we could work even faster, not havin' to keep an eye on her. By early afternoon, we each had a pile of finished stems in front of us. Ma's pile was as big as Maureen's and mine put together. I figured Ma's fingers were nimble from her sewin'. At this rate, we should be able to make good money, all of us workin' together like this. It wouldn't be long before we could get our own apartment and support ourselves.

I checked the clock. "It's one-thirty already. We'd better stop soon. Hildegarde and Trudy usually get home from school by two-thirty."

"Ye're right," Ma said. "Elsa and Friedrich will be comin' home with them today. I'm sure she wouldn't take kindly to havin' her table covered up with our mess."

"It's not a mess," Maureen said. "It's . . ."

Maureen never got the chance to finish her sentence, because at that moment the door opened, and I heard a scream.

Elsa, Hildegarde, Trudy, and a young man I surmised was Trudy's beau stood open-mouthed just inside the door. It didn't take long to figure out that Trudy had been the one doing the screamin', because, next thing I knew, she crumpled to the floor in a heap.

"Look what you've done to my sister!" Hildegarde screeched.

The beau gathered Trudy up in his arms and deposited her on the sofa in the front parlor. "Shall I get her some water, Mrs. Nolan?" he asked.

Ma started to answer, but when she realized she wasn't the Mrs. Nolan he had spoken to, she pretended to cough.

Elsa put her hand on his shoulder and pushed him toward the door. "I'll take care of her, Walter. It's best you leave now."

Walter took one look over his shoulder and did as he was told. Elsa ran to the sink to wet a washcloth, then held it to Trudy's forehead. Hildegarde patted her sister's hand and glared at us.

Trudy's eyelids fluttered open right away. I was sure she had been fakin' the whole time. Then her eyes widened and focused on us. "I just want to die! Walter saw these . . . these . . . immigrants running a sweatshop in our home. I'm so humiliated. He'll never want to marry me now."

"Nonsense," Ma said. "We were just workin' on a little project. There was no harm in it. No need to take on so."

Trudy let out a wail. "Mother. Pleeeease! Get rid of them."

"This has gone far enough," Elsa said. "I really don't know how much more we can take."

She got Trudy to her feet and helped her into the girls' bedroom. Hildegarde started to follow, then stopped in front of Ma. "You're in for it now. When Papa comes home, he's going to throw you out on the street, where you belong."

She stood there with her hands on her hips and a prissy smile on her face. Her pudgy cheeks were framed with two coiled braids, which made her look like someone had just taken her head out of the oven with potholders. I wanted to smack that face so hard her head would spin, but I never got the chance, because Maureen went by me in a blur.

She grabbed Hildegarde by her potholder braids and dragged her down to the floor. Then she pulled on the braids, poppin' hairpins all over the floor, and tied them together right in Hildegarde's mouth like a gag. I knew that we had just crossed some sort of line here and that there was big trouble ahead, but seein' that little brat on the floor silenced by her own hair was as sweet a moment as I'd had since steppin' off the boat.

Ma seemed to be enjoyin' the entertainment, too, and hadn't made a move to call Maureen off. As fate would have it, that's just the moment when Uncle Patrick came home, and all hell broke loose.

Poor Bridget didn't understand what all the yellin' was about, so she added her own bawlin' to the din. I could tell right from the beginnin' that this was a battle we had already lost, so I just held my breath and watched.

Elsa hauled Uncle Patrick into the bedroom, and we could hear all three female voices shoutin' at once.

Maureen came over to the table and hugged Ma. "I'm sorry I went after Hildegarde, Ma. I just couldn't help myself."

Ma tried to look stern, but her lips twitched into a smile. "Well, I don't condone fightin', but that girl's been askin' to have her braids stuffed in her mouth ever since we got here. I couldn't have done a better job myself."

16

When all the yellin' was over, Uncle Patrick came out of the bedroom with a sad look in his eyes. He poured a cup of coffee for himself and one for Ma, and motioned for her to sit at the table with him. At first she jutted out her chin and started to say somethin', but then she thought better of it and joined him.

"Things were easier in Limerick," he said. "I miss the Island Parish. Remember how we all used to play on Thomond Bridge when we were children?"

With the big fight that had gone on, now he was goin' to reminisce about Limerick? I couldn't believe my ears.

When Ma didn't say anything, he went on. "And all those games of king-of-the-castle on the steps of St. John's? How many children get to have a real castle as a playground?"

Ma smiled. "Or a real ghost for a playmate?"

She was talkin' about the Bishop's Lady, a ghost who was supposed to haunt Thomond Bridge. It was said that anyone who dared cross alone at night risked bein' thrown in the River Shannon by the angry she-ghost. We all grew up knowin' exactly where to find the marks made by the Bishop's Lady's fingers on the stone parapet. Even after I was old enough to know the story was just a *pishrogue*— a superstition—I couldn't bring myself to cross Thomond Bridge alone, day or night.

Ma and Uncle Patrick were still sharin' memories. "I loved watchin' the swans in the river," Ma said. I saw a quick picture in my mind of Ma's sad face lookin' over the bridge when I was little. Had she been mournin' her own lost childhood?

Uncle Patrick got up to pour more coffee. "We were lucky to live in the Island Parish instead of the lanes. At least we had food on the table, and enough coal for heat in the winter."

I knew what he meant. The very poorest people lived in the lanes of Limerick. They were crowded into small, damp stone houses, and most of them were on the dole.

As Ma and my uncle talked, scenes from Limerick tumbled through my mind. How strange to think that they had played the same games I had as a child. It was hard to picture them bein' young.

Maureen, who had been cowerin' in the corner of the parlor, went into the kitchen and took a seat next to Ma. I thought she was pushin' her luck. Ma and Uncle Patrick might have forgotten the fight for the moment, but it wasn't too bright of Maureen to be remindin' them by comin' out in plain sight like that. There wasn't a sound from the bedroom, but I was sure three pairs of ears were tryin' to pick up every word from the kitchen.

Finally, Uncle Patrick took a deep breath and leaned back in his chair. "There's no way around this, Margaret. It's not workin' out to have yer family here. I'll find another place for ye to stay. I can pay yer expenses until Michael gets back and settled with a job."

This was more than we could have hoped for. Uncle Patrick would take care of us until Da came back, but we wouldn't be stuck with his awful family. For once, I was grateful for Maureen's temper. She had brought everything to a head.

But then Ma ruined everything with one sentence. "That's very kind of ye, Patrick, but I've had enough of this country. I miss my husband and my baby somethin' terrible. We're like fish floppin' on a beach here. If we stay any longer, we'll perish for sure."

I jumped out of my chair. "But, Ma! We've just barely got here. Surely we should stay until Da comes back."

"And for what?" Ma asked. "Just so's he can put his heels on American soil and get right on the ship again?"

"Da wouldn't want to leave America," Maureen said. "All he could talk about was comin' here."

"And he isn't the one who has seen what it's like, now, is

he? He never got beyond Ellis Island, so I guess I'm the one who knows what America is all about."

"But, Margaret," Uncle Patrick said, "ye haven't given this country a chance."

Ma stood up. "Ye're a fine one to talk about givin' chances, Patrick Nolan. Ye think yer lovely wife and daughters cared a fig about givin' us a chance, do ye?"

Uncle Patrick raised his hands as if in surrender. "Now, don't get goin' on that again, Margaret. If leavin' is what ye want, I'll go right now and make arrangements. I don't want it said that I held ye here against yer will." He grabbed his coat and hat and was gone.

After the door slammed, the house was like two armed camps in an uneasy cease-fire. We could hear low murmurs from the bedroom, but Elsa and the girls stayed inside. Maureen and I pleaded with Ma to come to her senses, whisperin' in the far corner of the parlor. Ma suddenly put her head down on her arms and started to cry. I had to lean close to make out her muffled words. "I just can't take any more of this. I want my husband. And who knows what's become of poor Joseph? The family should be together. We had a good life in Limerick. We never should have left."

This frightened me. I couldn't remember ever seeing Ma cry in Ireland, even when her mother died, and then her father a year later. Through all that she had been strong as a ship's mast, but now she was weak and broken and cryin' at the drop of a hat. It didn't seem fair to argue with her, so I just rubbed her back and told her everything would be all right.

Uncle Patrick was back in less than an hour with tickets for a ship that would sail early the next mornin'. I could see that in America a politician could make things happen quickly. He said he had sent a telegram to Da in care of Grandma Nolan, tellin' them we were comin' home to Ireland. After that, we all had a sleepless night.

I tried to remember back when Da first started talkin' about comin' to America. It was mostly about the work. Da was a good provider and always managed to find jobs, even when some of the other men couldn't. Da was a coal man, fillin' his bags at Sutton's coal yard on the docks and deliverin' them to his customers by horse cart. It was hard work, and he was so covered with coal dust when he got home, Ma made him wash his head under the pump in the yard before he came into the house.

Ma and Da had both grown up in the Island Parish and had settled there after they were married. It wasn't really an island—just a neighborhood cut off from the rest of Limerick by a loop of the River Shannon. We never had a day of hunger or lacked for the simple comforts of life, but there was no money for extras, like a roast once in a while for Sunday dinner, or nicer clothes. Da thought he could make a better life for us in America, where his brother had arrived with twenty dollars and had climbed his way up from a dockworker to a politician.

I hadn't wanted to leave at first, but then I looked around at the girls who were a few years older than me. Most of them left school by the time they were my age, and after that there was nothin' for them but to marry. Bridey O'Flynn lived in the house across the street. She was four years older than me and already had two babies, with another on the way. She had been the most beautiful girl in the Parish when we were growin' up, but now she looked tired and old enough to be my mother.

I figured I had a lot of years to be raisin' babies and I wasn't in any great hurry to be gettin' started with it. And the worst of it was, even if I had a mind to be marryin' at a young age, most of the boys in Limerick didn't have the brains God gave a turnip, except for Dennis O'Reilly, who always knew the answers to the nuns' questions in school. There was only one small thing wrong with Dennis O'Reilly. He blossomed out with boils and carbuncles so often, I thought his insides must be packed full of pus just lookin' for a way to get out of him.

No, I wasn't goin' to settle for that. Da had said there were more Irishmen in New York than in Limerick and Dublin put together. And from what I had seen, they were doin' pretty well for themselves here, with their jobs as policemen and politicians. When the time came, I'd have my pick of an Irish husband, but for now, I had better things planned for myself. The more I thought about the boys and girls my age who were left at home, the more I resolved to talk Ma into stayin' here. I tried to keep awake to figure out a plan, but I must have fallen asleep, because I had a dream that I was in a room full of squallin' babies. And they all looked like Dennis O'Reilly, each with a little red boil set like a jewel right in the middle of its forehead.

Saturday mornin', Uncle Patrick offered to take us to the ship, but Ma wouldn't hear of it. "I'm sure we've been far too much trouble already," she said.

Uncle Patrick followed us out to the street. He tried to carry the trunk for Ma, but she had a death grip on it. Elsa and the others didn't get up to say goodbye, which was probably a good thing. When we reached the street, Uncle Patrick hailed a carriage for us. He lifted Ma and placed her in the seat, then pressed some money into the driver's hand and told him which pier to take us to. Ma had the good sense not to argue. It was cold and not yet light.

Uncle Patrick kissed me on the cheek. "I'm sorry we got off to a bad start, Rose. If ye come back, I'll make sure things are different." He helped me into the seat, then lifted up Maureen and Bridget. I turned to wave as we started off. He looked so sad standin' there. I wondered if he longed to go back to Ireland with us, or if he was sad to see us missin' out on a chance to be Americans.

I looked around, tryin' to take in every sight as we headed for the docks. What an amazin' city this was—so many people all goin' about their lives. It seemed there were more immigrants livin' here than native-born Americans. And some of them had come over here with less than we had. I knew that for sure. I had seen them on the boat, and in the streets, and in that sweatshop where we made roses. Roses! I had forgotten to return the stems to Mr. Moscovitz. "Ma! What happened to the stems?"

"Good Lord, Rose, it makes no matter now."

"Did we leave them at Uncle Patrick's?"

"No, I didn't want to leave a trace of us there for Elsa to complain about. I put them in the suitcase, not that you'll have any use for them."

I pulled the valise up on my lap and opened it. There, under my dress of ashes of roses, was the small paper-bound package. That made me feel better.

As soon as we could finish them, I'd take them back to Mr. Moscovitz's shop. Even though Uncle Patrick said he'd pay our expenses, we could send any money we earned to Da to help him come back sooner. I knew we could ask Uncle Patrick for the fare, but Da was a proud man and probably wouldn't accept it.

I looked at Ma's face and tried to figure how hard it would be to convince her to stay. She had pulled Bridget onto her lap and was nuzzlin' the top of her head, the way she always did with her babies. I knew she was thinkin' about Joseph. That would be the hardest thing—convincin' Ma that Joseph could do without her.

The carriage took us all the way across Twelfth Street. There were so many buildings here, stretchin' as far as I could see. A carriage ride of a few minutes in Limerick would have us out into the countryside, but here the city seemed to have no end. Lights were just beginnin' to go on as people got ready for work. We rode in silence. I wanted to plead with Ma to stay, but I thought I might have better luck if I took her by surprise at the last minute. If I started now, she'd knock down a hundred of my arguments by the time we reached the pier.

Suddenly we had reached the end of New York and saw the Hudson River spread out in front of us. Several huge oceanliners were lined up in their berths, the same as they had been when we arrived in New York. That was only two weeks ago, but it seemed like we had lived a whole lifetime since then. I realized Da's ship must be just about arrivin' in Cork.

We pulled up alongside a big steamer, and the driver unloaded our goods. It was now or never. I took a deep breath and blurted it out. "Ma, please, let's stay. Let's take up Uncle Patrick on his offer for a nice little place of our own."

Maureen stared at me with her mouth open. Ma hiked Bridget on her hip and picked up the valise. "Nonsense, Rose. We're not stayin' in this terrible place, and that's the end of it."

I took hold of Ma's arm to stop her. "Then let me stay. You take the girls and go back, but let me have the money from my ticket and I'll make my own way until you and Da come back. Uncle Patrick doesn't have to know."

"Don't be ridiculous. Ye're a child. Surely ye don't think I'll let ye stay here by yerself."

"I'm not a child, Ma. Back home, some of my friends are married women already."

"With husbands to take care of them, I'll remind ye." Ma shook loose from my grip. "Not wanderin' around in a strange city by themselves."

I stood my ground. "I won't be alone. I'll find a job and a place to stay. I'll either go back to the rose-makin' shop, or I'll find another job where I can use my sewin' skills."

"You heard what Elsa said about the sweatshops. That's no place for a decent girl to work." Ma had to move out of the way for a porter pushin' a wagon of luggage. More and more carriages were pullin' up now, and a large crane was swingin' pallets of cargo on board.

Maureen jumped in. "Oh, Ma, Elsa doesn't know what she's talkin' about. Rose can take care of herself."

Ma jutted out her chin. "So ye think she'll make her way with her fists, like you, Maureen? The answer is still no."

I had never openly defied my parents before, unlike Maureen, who had some objection to every rule they laid down. But now I had no choice. I couldn't make myself go back to Ireland.

Ma picked up the feather bed. "You and Maureen take the trunk. I need to hold Bridget. Lord knows there's enough places a child can get lost here."

I pulled on her sleeve again. "Ma, please! Don't ye remember how awful it was comin' over in steerage? I've just barely got the stink of it out of my nose. I can't do that again."

"Ye can stop yer complaints right now, Rose. Patrick got us accommodations in second-class. It'll be a far cry from the trip over here. Ye're lucky yer uncle can pull a few strings with the Democratic Party."

The crowd was beginnin' to get thick as more carriages discharged their passengers on the pier. The gangplank to the huge steamer was now a solid mass of movin' bodies.

"Ma!" I pleaded one more time. "Please let me stay. The money for a second-class ticket will give me a good start. I can get a nice place to stay while I look for a job."

Ma's face was red with anger. "I'll not argue with ye. If yer father were here, ye wouldn't be standin' up to him like this."

"Yes, I would, Ma. This means a lot to me, and I'm not arguin', either. I'm just stayin'. And that's final." I couldn't stop myself now. The words poured out of me as if somebody else were doin' the talkin'. "If ye won't give me back my ticket, then I'll manage anyway. I'll live on the streets if I have to until I get a job. Now I'll help ye get our goods onto the boat, but then I'm gettin' off."

"Look what this place has done to ye already," Ma shouted over the din of the crowd. "I don't even know ye anymore. My own daughter has turned against me."

Seein' her tears again shook my resolve, but I stood firm. I held out my hand. "Give me the ticket, Ma."

She glared at me with that look that always made me give in. I lifted my chin and returned the stare. We kept our eyes locked even when the crowd jostled us. Then, unbelievably, Ma blinked and looked away. Never in my whole life had I ever been able to stare down my mother. She pulled out a ticket and handed it to me. "I don't have the strength to wrestle ye onto the boat, Rose. Open the suitcase and take out Maureen's extra dress and shawl. The rest of it is yours."

Maureen moved to my side. "If Rose stays, then I'm staying, too."

Why did she have to speak up now and ruin everything? "I can't be havin' ye with me, Maureen. It'll be enough for me to take care of myself."

Maureen looked up at me, and I could see in her face the same desperation I felt in not wantin' to go back. "But I'll be company for ye, Rose. And I can work at home makin' those stems, so it won't cost ye anything to have me here. I'll earn my own way."

Ma grabbed her arm. "Don't be foolish, Maureen. A child yer age needs to be in school."

"Then I'll work after school."

Ma let go of Maureen and shouted at the sky. "Ye see what ye've done to me, America? Ye've taken my two sweet daughters and turned them into headstrong fools. What will ye do to me next?" Bridget, who had been lookin' back and forth at us, started to wail.

A man next to Ma put his arm around his wife as if to protect her from the crazy woman with the bawlin' child.

Could I leave Ma like this? Would she be all right? The great ship blew its horn, which almost made me jump out of my skin. It seemed to snap Ma back to her senses. She rummaged in her purse and pulled out a second ticket. "I don't know what's right or wrong anymore, but ye're both so stubborn, I'm washin' my hands of the both of ye." She slapped the second ticket into my hand. "Who knows? Maybe ye'll be better off with the two of ye here than with Rose by herself."

I couldn't utter a word, afraid that anything I might say could cause Ma to snatch back the tickets and make an even bigger scene to embarrass us into goin' with her.

Suddenly fear gripped me. It was one thing to stand up on my hind legs and demand to stay here, but now it was really happenin', and Ma was lettin' Maureen stay, too. Did I know how to take care of us?

Ma gave me a hug, then held me at arm's length to look at me, tears streamin' down her cheeks. "Promise me this. Ye'll go back to yer Uncle Patrick's and stay with them. I'll not have ye livin' on yer own."

"Yes, Ma."

"And ye'll write me a letter every day. Every single day without fail."

"We will, Ma," Maureen said. "We'll write all the time."

Ma wiped her nose on the back of her hand. "And ye'll get yerselves into school. Both of ye."

"Yes, Ma," I said. We carried the trunk and feather bed over to the gangplank. She gave the man her tickets, and a crewman hoisted the trunk to his shoulders and started to pick up the feather bed.

Ma stopped him. "Wait! Give the feather bed to my girls."

I knew how much that bed meant to Ma. "No, Ma. It's all right. Take it for yerself."

She pushed it into my arms. "If I'm leavin' ye alone in this country, I want the comfort of knowin' ye're not sleepin' on a cold, hard floor. I doubt those girls would share the beds in their room with ye."

She started toward the gangplank with Bridget, then stopped and ran back to us, Bridget bouncin' on her hip like a rag doll. Holy Mother of God! Had she changed her mind?

I braced myself for the worst, but she only said, "Ye must turn in yer tickets right away, so ye can give the money back to Uncle Patrick. They may not give ye a refund if ye wait till we've sailed."

I nodded. "All right, Ma."

She wiped a tear from my cheek. "Ye may be Rose in America, but to me ye'll always be Margaret Rose." She gave Maureen a quick hug, then before I could say anything else she disappeared into the crush of people.

Another blast from the steamer's horn made me jump, and I heard a man on board shout, "All ashore who's going ashore." Two tugboats had moved into position by the huge steamer. People were comin' down the gangplank now, and those who were sailin' found places along the rail. I looked for Ma, but couldn't see her.

Then I remembered the tickets. "Hurry up, Maureen." I saw the ticket booth and started runnin' for it, the feather bed thuddin' against my knees. I reached the window just as the ticket seller was ready to close. "Please, sir," I gasped. "We've decided not to sail."

He scowled at me. "I could have sold these just two minutes ago."

He took the tickets, opened a metal box, counted out some bills and coins, and shoved them under the metal grate. I opened the valise and tucked the money into a corner.

Maureen tugged at my sleeve. "Let's go wave to Ma and Bridget."

As we pushed our way through the crowd, the ship gave three more blasts, and the tugs added their horns to the commotion. "It's movin'," Maureen cried. "Where's Ma?"

"I don't know. We're too far back to see the faces."

Maureen ducked her head and pushed through the crowd like a billy goat, draggin' me along, bowlin' people over with the feather bed. We finally arrived at the front, leavin' a path of irate people in our wake.

I searched along the ship's rail until I saw Ma. "There!" I pointed.

We waved frantically, but Ma didn't see us. She had that same sad expression I had seen years ago on Thomond Bridge. Was she mournin' her lost daughters this time?

Maureen's next words gave me a chill. "Do ye think Ma is plannin' to come back to America?"

I couldn't give her an answer.

"Maybe Da won't come back, either."

"Don't worry about it." I could barely speak over the sob that was lodged in my throat. The fishy smell of the water reminded me of the Limerick docks. I saw a rope danglin' down the side of the ship, and for one frantic moment I considered jumpin' for it and climbin' up to the safety of my mother's arms. But then I remembered I'd be headin' for a future with Dennis O'Reilly and a houseful of ugly babies.

Maureen looked up at the ship. "Do ye think we'll be all right?"

I turned and hugged her so she couldn't see my face. I couldn't say for sure that we'd be all right, but I knew one thing. I had absolutely no intention of goin' back to Uncle Patrick's.

17

With the money from our tickets, Maureen and I set off to find a place to stay. I knew better than to inquire in the fancy areas. We could probably get more money from Uncle Patrick if we had to, but I didn't want to give Elsa and her daughters the satisfaction of seein' us beg.

The street sign across from the pier said West Tenth Street. I grabbed Maureen's hand and started off.

"Are we walkin' all the way back to Uncle Patrick's?" Maureen asked.

"We're not goin' to Uncle Patrick's."

Maureen smiled. "I was hopin' ye'd say that."

I was tryin' to get my bearings. I knew that the Hudson River was on the West Side of the city, and we needed to be on the East Side, near the East River. I also knew we had to head down through the streets with lower numbers, and that the street numbers got lower as they went south. I turned right at the next corner.

"Do ye know where ye're goin'?" Maureen asked.

"Of course. The next street will be Ninth Street," I said, feelin' smug.

When we reached the corner, Maureen said, "That's a funny way to spell 'Ninth.'" It was Christopher Street.

"It's all right," I said. The next street was Barrow, then Morton. I decided to start walkin' across town and got us into a maze of narrow streets, not a numbered one among 'em. Maureen was keepin' up a steady stream of questions, such as how did I know we were goin' the right way, and where were we goin' anyway? I was just about to admit we were lost when we stumbled upon West Houston Street. I knew that name. I had crossed East Houston on the way to Mr. Moscovitz's shop. It was the first street below the numbered streets on the East Side. Now all I needed to do was follow it until I came to something I recognized. I stepped out with confidence at last.

"This looks like a nice neighborhood," Maureen said. "Why don't we find a place to stay here?"

"I want to be close to the place where they make roses. We'll look on Broome Street. We can afford the rent there."

"Are we both goin' to work now?" Maureen asked. "I'm not afraid, ye know. I'm not a ninny like Hildegarde and Trudy."

"No. I promised Ma ye'd stay in school."

"Ye promised her we'd go to Uncle Patrick's, too. I don't see that happenin'."

"All right. Maybe ye can work on the flowers at night at home."

"Maybe I could work durin' the day and do my studies at night at home."

"We'll see," I said. I knew it was senseless to argue with her. Better to humor her until I couldn't hide the truth any longer. She was goin' to school if I had to drag her there every mornin' and chain her to a school desk. I'd not have her growin' up ignorant. I knew one thing. To make yer way in this country, ye needed to be smart.

Just as I was startin' to worry about gettin' lost again, we came to the Bowery. "We're almost there," I said, turnin' the corner and walkin' faster. Maureen was enchanted by it all. "So many people. Did ye ever see so many people in one place?" The usual crush of pushcarts and peddler wagons was startin' to clog up the street.

When we turned onto Broome Street, I spotted a "room for rent" sign about halfway down the first block. We went inside and inquired, but the owner said he wanted to rent to a man, not two girls. I thought that was odd, but after three more landlords tellin' us the same thing, I was beginnin' to get discouraged.

"Maybe we should start askin' people in the street if they want to rent out their closet," Maureen said. "I'm tired and hungry, Rose. Can't we stop to eat?"

There were some peddlers' wagons on West Broadway, so we stopped to buy a loaf of black bread. Maureen ripped herself off a huge hunk, but I took the piece from her and broke it in two. "Don't be greedy," I said, keepin' half for myself. "This has to last us a while."

After walkin' two more blocks, Maureen spotted a sign on a side street named Sullivan, but we couldn't read it until we got up close. "Room for rent. See Garoff, second floor, rear."

"Let me do the talkin'," I said as we ran up the stairs. There were only two apartments on the second floor.

An odd-lookin' man opened the rear door when I knocked. He reminded me of the immigrants at Ellis Island, with his black hat and threadbare black suit. He gave me a puzzled look. "You want something?"

"You have a room to rent?" I asked.

The man said nothin'—just looked at me in an odd way.

"There was a sign outside," I said. "Room to rent. Are you Mr. Garoff?"

"I was looking for a young man. Jewish."

"We wouldn't be any trouble," I said. "We're quiet, and we can take care of ourselves."

Mr. Garoff shook his head. "I already have my daughter to look after. I don't need more girls."

Maureen pushed in front of me. "My sister told ye, we don't need lookin' after. We're perfectly able to fend for ourselves. We just need a place to stay."

Mr. Garoff sighed. "Already I have one girl with a big mouth, and now this."

I heard Maureen take in a breath as if she were about to say somethin' else, so I pulled her behind me before she could open her mouth.

I gave Mr. Garoff my most charmin' smile. "My sister didn't mean anything, sir. Could we perhaps meet yer daughter?" I thought if she were our age, she might be on our side.

"She won't be home until after seven. You come back then and we talk about this."

Seven. It would be dark by then, and the little warmth the sun was givin' us now would be gone. If he decided then that we couldn't stay, we'd be out in the cold for the night. I had to convince him. "Please, Mr. Garoff. We need a place to stay tonight. We'll pay for the one night, and if ye want us to leave tomorrow, we'll go. Just, please, let us sleep here tonight. It's freezin' outside."

He rubbed his beard and scowled at Maureen.

"I apologize for my outburst, sir," Maureen said, knowin' she had put us in this predicament. "I'm mostly very quiet."

I bit my lip to keep from laughin'. Maureen wasn't accustomed to apologies.

Mr. Garoff sighed. "All right. Come. I show you the room. You pay just for one night. Then we see if you stay after that. Maybe, maybe not." He raised his eyebrows at Maureen, who ducked her head meekly and followed us into the apartment.

"We have one extra room. And when my wife and other daughters come from Russia, you leave . . . if you are still here then."

There was one square room, with a woodstove and a table. The room itself was the same shape as the main room in Uncle Patrick's, only much smaller, and there was no parlor leadin' into it. I could see a dark bedroom off the back of the room, and a cot in the main room looked like someone slept there, too. Mr. Garoff pulled back a curtain that led into a tiny room with no furniture. Maureen had joked about livin' in a closet, but it appeared that was exactly the space Mr. Garoff had for rent. "It's not large," he said, as if we were blind.

I countered with, "It's fine," before Maureen could put in her two cents' worth.

Mr. Garoff nodded. "Make yourselves comfortable. Tonight, after you meet my daughter Gussela, we'll see."

"Thank you," I said.

"Oh, and one other thing. No food."

"No food?" Maureen cried. "We can't eat in our own room?"

Mr. Garoff scowled. "You eat your own food. You don't eat mine. No food goes with price of room."

"Oh," Maureen said. "That's fine. We'll buy our own food."

Mr. Garoff shrugged. "Just so we understand each other."

I closed our curtain and plumped the feather bed against the wall to give us a place to sit. We wouldn't need chairs, even if there was room for them, which there wasn't. The stove in the next room sent its warmth directly into our room, and the one tiny window seemed to be sealed tight so there were no drafts on the floor. Maureen and I sat next to each other on the bed.

"We have our own place in America," she whispered. "It's not much, but it's ours."

"For tonight," I reminded her. "And now we have to work on our stems. Mr. Moscovitz will be angry at me for not bringin' them back today. I need to take them back finished, tomorrow."

We bent our heads close to the fading light from the window. "It gets dark too early now. Tomorrow I'll buy a candle."

Mr. Garoff must have heard us, for he knocked on the frame of the door. "If you need light, I have extra oil lamp. It could be part of the rent."

I pulled back the curtain and took the lighted lamp. "Thank you."

"Don't burn midnight oil," he said. "I'm not a wealthy man."

I set the lamp on the floor, and its light filled the whole room. Now it was much easier to see what we were doin'. We took a short break to have a little more bread for our supper, then went back to work.

It wasn't long before we had quite a pile of finished stems between us. I started out checkin' every one that Maureen made, but when I found that hers were every bit as good as mine, I stopped checkin' and just kept workin'.

"What are ye goin' to tell Ma, Rose?"

"Why should I tell her anything?"

"Ye have to. When ye write to her."

"I'm not goin' to write until I have somethin' good to say."

"But havin' a place is good," Maureen protested. "Besides, ye promised to write every day."

"Just like I promised to go to Uncle Patrick's," I said, makin' a joke of it. But deep inside it hurt me to be breakin' a promise to my own mother.

We heard someone come in, and a young woman's voice joined Mr. Garoff's low grumbly one.

"That must be his daughter," Maureen whispered. "Should we go out and meet her?"

"I don't know. Maybe we should wait till we're invited." I'd never lived in another person's house, except for Uncle Patrick's, and that didn't count because it was family. If we hadn't been welcome with our own relatives, how would it be with strangers? I wondered why Mr. Garoff wanted to talk over our staying here with his daughter. Surely he would be the one to make the decision.

My thoughts were interrupted by Gussela callin' out near our door curtain. "Hello! Would you like to join us for some tea?"

Maureen and I scrambled to our feet. I smoothed down my hair before we went out.

Gussela was pourin' tea into a glass. "*Glezel tai,* Papa?"

He nodded, and she placed the glass in front of him, then poured some for us. She had strong features, with beautiful large, brown eyes. Her dark hair was pulled back and knotted at the nape of her neck. She looked up. "Come sit. I'm Gussie. Papa has told me you want to rent our room, but he didn't tell me your names."

I quickly introduced us as we took our places at the table, realizin' that Mr. Garoff had never asked us who we were.

"Nolan?" Gussie said. "You're from Ireland, no?" She sounded American, with none of the heavy accent of her father.

I nodded. "From Limerick. We've not been here very long."

"There aren't many Irish in this neighborhood. Not more than one or two Irish girls at work that I can think of." Gussie took a seat next to her father.

I wasn't goin' to say anything about our situation, but Maureen blurted out about Da havin' to go back with Joseph and how we stayed with Uncle Patrick but Ma didn't like it here and went back. She talked so fast I didn't get a chance to kick her under the table before she'd gone through our whole life story.

"It's brave of you to stay here on your own," Gussie said.

"We have work," Maureen said. "Makin' parts of flowers." Before I could stop her, she jumped up and brought one of our stems from the room.

Gussie turned it over in her fingers. "Where do you do this?"

"The shop is over on Chrystie Street," I said, "but Mr. Moscovitz let me take work home. Don't worry, we won't make a mess. We're very careful."

"Gussela is a seamstress," Mr. Garoff said. "She has good job at shirtwaist factory on Washington Square."

"Is that where they make those pretty Gibson Girl blouses?" Maureen asked.

"It's one of the places," Gussie said. "Probably the largest. Our company takes up the top three floors of the building. Over four hundred people work there."

I couldn't imagine workin' in a place that large. No wonder Gussie seemed so sophisticated. Her job made ours seem childish. Still, I wasn't sure I'd have the courage to apply for a job in a big factory even if they'd take me.

Gussie got up to pour more tea into our glasses, servin' her father first. "This tea not usual," Mr. Garoff said.

"It's very good," I said, thinkin' he meant this was somethin' special served in our honor.

Mr. Garoff leaned toward me. "I mean you not usually drink *our* tea. You get your own tea."

Gussie laughed. "Oh, Papa. A few extra tea leaves won't put us into the poorhouse."

"Why rent out room if it costs money instead of bringing money?" he said.

"We can buy our own tea," Maureen said. "We like Irish tea, anyway."

"Do you use one of those machines for your sewin'?" I asked, hopin' to distract them from Maureen's rudeness.

Gussie slipped back into her place at the table. "Yes, it makes the work go much faster."

"Our mother is a seamstress," I said, "but she does everything by hand." Thinking that made her sound backward, I added, "She makes dresses for a fancy shop in Limerick."

"She must be very patient," Gussie said.

I thought about that. "Patient" was not a word I'd use to describe Ma, but I let it go.

We managed an awkward conversation until our glasses were empty. Gussie was friendly enough, but she seemed to regard us with curiosity, and her father's glares made it clear that he wasn't pleased to have us as renters. Finally, we excused ourselves to go back to work. I thanked Gussie for the tea, and she said, "I hope you'll enjoy living here."

I smiled at Maureen. That meant that some sort of decision had been made over our little tea party. We had found a place to stay, at least until the rest of the Garoff family came over from Russia.

I relit the lamp, and Maureen and I counted out the stems in bunches of ten. For all our hard work, we had only managed to make 1,247 stems. We worked another hour, but when Mr. Garoff made a comment purposely loud enough for us to hear about the cost of lamp oil, we extinguished the light and went to bed.

"We'll get up at dawn," I whispered to Maureen. "Maybe

we can finish the rest so I can take them back in the mornin'."

"Is the shop open on Sunday?"

"I forgot what day it was. We just need to have them ready on Monday, then."

Sunday mornin', Gussie told us where to find a Catholic church. I figured lyin' to Ma about stayin' at Uncle Patrick's was bad enough. The very least I could do was get myself and Maureen to Mass.

We started right in on the stems when we got home, but we barely had all three thousand stems bundled up and ready by bedtime that night.

"My fingers are sore from bendin' the wire," Maureen complained. "How are we goin' to do this day after day?"

I looked at the red stripes on my own fingers. "Maybe we'll get calluses," I said. "It must get easier. Nobody would do this job if it stayed so painful."

"They would if they wanted to eat," Maureen said. Before I could come up with an encouragin' thought, she had fallen asleep sittin' up on the feather bed, leanin' against the wall.

18

First thing Monday mornin', I headed for Mr. Moscovitz's shop with the finished stems. Maureen had whined about goin' along with me, but I didn't want her to cause problems.

A dusting of snow had fallen durin' the night, makin' the sidewalks slippery as I walked along. The girls were just settlin' in at the tables when I got there. Mr. Moscovitz looked up. "Ah, so the little thief has returned."

I handed him the bundle of stems. "I didn't steal them. It just took longer than I expected to do them."

He opened the bundle, dumped the stems on the table, and started tossin' some of them aside.

"What are you doin'?" I asked.

"I'm throwing out the bad ones," he said. "You don't expect me to pay for stems I can't use, do you?"

"If you show me what's wrong with them, I'll fix them."

Mr. Moscovitz kept addin' to the discard pile. "I'm running a business here, not a school."

I picked up one of the rejected stems and looked it over, but I couldn't see a thing wrong with it. I remembered what Mr. Moscovitz had said about me being charged for the materials on the stems I had ruined. I could see the money for our hard work slippin' away with each stem he rejected.

"Please, Mr. Moscovitz," I said quietly. "I really need the work now. My mother and youngest sister have gone back to Ireland. I have to earn the money to take care of me and my sister Maureen."

Mr. Moscovitz raised his eyebrows at this remark, but said nothin'.

Laughter came from the workers' table. I had spoken so quietly to Mr. Moscovitz, I was sure they couldn't have heard me. Tessa had just said somethin' to the others, and looked at me with a smirk on her face. How had I ever thought she might be a friend? Wasn't there anyone I could trust in this country?

Mr. Moscovitz shoved the stems aside. "It will take too long to sort these out now. You come back tonight, after the shop closes, and I'll give you the pay you deserve. Not a cent less . . . or more."

"What time is that?" I asked, rememberin' that I had left early the day I worked here.

"Come at eight," he said.

I left the shop feelin' helpless. I had hoped to go home with money in my pocket. Now I knew Mr. Moscovitz could pay me as little as he pleased, and I had no way to fight it. The thought occurred to me that I might be better off workin' at the shop again, instead of takin' work home. That way there would be witnesses to what I had produced, although I couldn't see any of the other girls stickin' up for me if I got into a dispute with Mr. Moscovitz. As far as they were concerned, I was an outsider, and not worth riskin' their jobs over.

When I got home, Maureen and I went out to buy tea and a pot to steep it in. They were both more expensive than I'd expected, but Mr. Garoff had made it clear that he wouldn't be sharin' his tea with us, so I had no choice. I had wanted to buy a knife for cuttin' bread, but decided that was a luxury we couldn't afford until I knew how much money we'd be makin' on a regular basis. Our small loaf was almost gone. I figured we might be able to get one more meal out of it, then we'd have to buy another. At least we had a room that was warm and dry, and that was somethin' to be thankful for.

I arrived at the shop that night just as the girls were leavin'. Tessa came over to me. "You're a fool to come back," she said. "That old goat won't give you a penny." Then she turned and ran to catch up to the others.

When I went into the shop, Mr. Moscovitz was hunched over his ledger book at the table. He barely glanced at me. "Sit down and wait. I'm busy."

I took a seat at the far end of the table. Two of the older women were wrappin' themselves up in scarves and talkin' in Russian or Polish, I couldn't tell which. One of them made a cluckin' sound with her tongue and shook her head as they shuffled by me on their way to the door. They were still angry at me for takin' work home? Well, so be it.

When the door shut behind the two women, Mr. Moscovitz closed his ledger and stood up, stretchin' his back. "Ah, the workday is over. Now is time to relax, no? Here, let me take your coat." He folded it, placed it carefully on the table, and smiled at me.

I felt a sense of relief. I smiled back at him.

He went over to the stove and poured two glasses of tea. He set one in front of me, then unwrapped a paper and pulled out two small pastries.

"This is the time of day I treat myself," he said. He ripped the paper into two "plates" and shoved one over next to my tea.

He leaned back in his chair and rubbed his hand over his big belly. "No need to rush, right? No one will worry if you're not home right away?"

"Well, there's my sister." I was startin' to feel uneasy.

He pulled a piece of sugar candy from his pocket and set it on the table. "You give this to your sister when you get home."

Mr. Moscovitz sipped his tea, watchin' me. "You know, I see many girls who come here for work. Many girls. Most don't have the good sense God gave them. But every now and then, I see a special girl. One like you, Rose."

I could feel myself blushin'.

Mr. Moscovitz took a big bite of pastry, spillin' sugar on his vest and tie, then talked with his mouth full. "I'm going to expand this shop, Rose, and I'll need someone to manage it for me. Of course, this won't happen right away, but maybe in another month or so. I'll need someone with a good head on her shoulders."

Was he offerin' me the job? I couldn't tell. Why would he pick me over someone like Tessa? I took a sip of tea, but could barely swallow.

"The job will pay well," he continued, leanin' toward me. "Very well. It could put your worries about caring for your sister to rest."

His face was so close to mine, I could see the sparkles of sugar on his lower lip and in his beard. Then, suddenly, he grabbed my shoulders and pulled me to my feet. Before I knew what was happenin', he had me pressed close to his chest and was kissin' me hard on the mouth. I struggled to get away, but he held both of my hands firmly behind my back. He slammed me down backward on the table, and I heard the glasses hit the floor and shatter. I managed to turn my face away from him and scream, but nobody came. Who would hear?

"Be smart," he shouted. "Think of your sister. You don't want her to starve, do you?"

All I knew at that moment was that I would rather have

Maureen and me cold in the ground than have this beast touch me. As he moved in to kiss me again, I clamped my teeth down on his nose. He let out a bellow and reeled back, knockin' over several chairs and fallin' to the floor.

I dove for the door and tried to open the latch, but my fingers wouldn't work right. All of a sudden Mr. Moscovitz was on his feet and headin' for me. I gave one hard yank, the door unlatched, and I burst outside.

I ran through the front building and out onto the street. My mind was racin'. I couldn't remember how to get back to the apartment. I reached the end of the block and didn't recognize the name of the street. Where was I? Had I run the wrong way? Was he followin' me? I looked back down the street. There was no sign of him.

My knees went weak. I leaned back against a wall, breathin' hard. The cold of the brick cut through my dress. My coat! I had left it at the shop. It was the middle of winter, and now I had no coat.

I licked my lips and tasted sugar. I hadn't taken a single bite of my pastry. I remembered Mr. Moscovitz's sugar-coated lips and sank to my knees. I vomited up every bite of food I'd had all day.

19

I was half froze by the time I found our apartment. Gussie and Mr. Garoff were sittin' at the table when I burst in. I ran past them into our little closet without sayin' a word.

Maureen had been nappin' but sat bolt upright when I flung myself down on the feather bed next to her. "Rose! What happened to ye?"

"Nothin'," I said, buryin' my face in the feather bed. It smelled like Ma and home. I wanted to wrap it around me like a cocoon and never come out again.

I could feel Maureen's fingers pokin' at my bare shoulder. "Rose, yer sleeve is partly ripped off. What happened?"

I started to sob. That awful man had ruined my dress.

Maureen gripped my shoulder now and tried to turn me over. "Rose, tell me what's wrong. Ye're scarin' me."

"Leave me alone!" I wailed. I couldn't tell her what had happened. How could I have been so stupid? Ma was right. I couldn't take care of myself, much less a younger sister.

I heard Maureen get up and leave. Then, a few minutes later, she was next to me again, pattin' my back. I turned over and swatted her hand away. But when I looked up, it wasn't Maureen. It was Gussie.

"I'm sorry," I gasped. "I thought ye were my sister."

"Shhhh." Gussie put her finger to her lips. "You don't have to say anything. I sent Maureen out with my father for a little while. There's not much privacy in these tight quarters, and I thought you could use a little time to yourself."

Maureen was alone with Mr. Garoff? I sat up. "No! I have to get my sister!"

I was all the way to the apartment door before Gussie caught my arm. "Wait! Are you afraid that my father will harm Maureen? Because, if you are, I can assure you he's a gentle and honorable man."

Gussie practically wrestled me over to the table and pushed me firmly into a chair. "You're not running out into the cold with no coat on. If you don't want to tell me what's wrong, that's fine. But at least drink a glass of tea and try to calm down."

I was shiverin' so hard, I could hardly bring the glass to my lips. Gussie sat across the table from me and watched. It didn't take long before I started tellin' her about what happened. I told how Moscovitz hadn't paid me the money for the stems earlier in the day, and how he wanted me to go back after the shop closed to get my pay.

"You were foolish to go there alone at night," she said.

"I don't need ye tellin' me that," I shouted. "I'm sick and tired of everybody pointin' out everything I do wrong. But my stupidity didn't give him the right to . . ." I couldn't even say the words.

"What did he do, Rose?"

I started cryin' again.

"Did he hurt you? Did he . . ."

"He kissed me," I cried, feelin' the revulsion all over.

"Is that all?"

"Is that all! He was a filthy, disgustin' old man! It was terrible!"

"I know. I know. I didn't mean to belittle what happened. You're just lucky that's all he did." She gave me her handkerchief. "I'm assuming you didn't get the money for your work tonight."

I shook my head and blew my nose.

Gussie banged her fist on the table, causing the glasses to clatter and me to jump like a nervous cat. "It makes me furious. We fought so hard for our rights, but the owners of these shops don't care. They just do as they please, and nobody stops them."

"What do ye mean about fightin'?" I asked, wipin' my nose.

Gussie looked at me as if I had half a brain. "The strikes, of course. Have you not heard about them?"

I was embarrassed to admit my ignorance. When I didn't answer, she came to her own conclusion. "I forgot. The strikes were two years ago. You were in Ireland, weren't you?" She rubbed her forehead. "How strange. It seemed like such a revolution to us, I would have thought the whole world knew."

"Ye went out on strike?"

"Yes. Hundreds of us. And not just in New York, either. We had girls go out in other cities, like Rochester and Philadelphia. The police beat us and threw us into jail. Look here." She pulled back the sleeve of her blouse, revealing a large lump on her wrist. "A policeman broke my arm with his nightstick and it never healed right. They wouldn't let me out of jail to see a doctor."

"Ye were in jail?" She looked so fragile, I couldn't imagine her standin' up to a policeman.

Gussie nodded. "Don't mention this around my father. It almost killed him to have his daughter in trouble with the law. This sort of thing just isn't done by women in the old country. Father thinks I should keep quiet, but when I see something wrong, I want to change it. Luckily, I'm not the only one who feels that way."

I was beginnin' to understand what Gussie's father meant about havin' one big-mouthed girl in the house. "I don't know how ye can be so brave," I said. "I'm not meek by any means, but I'd not stand up to a policeman with a stick, that's for sure."

"One person might not have the courage, Rose, but when there are hundreds, it's not so hard. Even if you get hurt or jailed, there are many to help. We even had the support of some of the most important women in New York. It's one thing to have poor working girls in a picket line, but when you have society ladies, well, that's a news story."

Gussie's cheeks were flushed with excitement. "I've been rattling on and not giving you a chance to talk. What are your plans, now that you won't be going back to the flower-making shop?"

She thought I had plans? I didn't have an idea in my head. "I guess I need to find another place to work."

"That's just what I was thinking. You have some sewing skills, right? Your mother was a seamstress in Ireland?"

"Well, yes, but I'm nowhere near as good as her."

"Do you know how to run a sewing machine?"

"No. I've never . . ."

"Don't worry. I can get a machine and some scrap material for you to practice on. Then, if you want, I'll talk to the foreman at work and see if he'll give you a job."

"Do ye think I could learn fast enough to get a factory job?"

"You know the answer to that question better than me, Rose."

I had my doubts, but I wasn't about to turn down a job. "There's just one other thing," I said.

"What's that?"

"Well, I have nothin' to wear."

"What you have on is fine," Gussie said. "You don't have to be fashionable to work at the Triangle, although some of the girls spend most of their paychecks trying to look like fine ladies. It makes more sense to wear serviceable clothes. After you get your first pay, I can take you to some shops that have good clothes for reasonable prices."

"No, it's not that," I said, when she finally took a breath. "I have no coat. If the factory is a distance away, I'll be too cold walkin' with just a dress on."

"For heaven's sake, Rose, what happened to your coat? Did you leave it at the shop?"

"Yes, I just ran."

"So not only does Moscovitz get your work for free, he gets a coat in the bargain?"

I nodded.

"We'll go back there first thing in the morning. We'll get your coat and your money."

"But ye'll be late for work. Won't ye get in trouble?"

"One of the neighbors works on my floor. I'll have her tell the foreman I'll be late." Gussie grinned. "Besides, I haven't had a good fight in a long time."

20

❧ *I stayed awake* half the night worryin' about bein' carted off to jail. Tuesday mornin', I expressed my concerns to Gussie.

"We're just going back there to get your coat, Rose. And the pay that Mr. Moscovitz owes you. He can't have us arrested for that."

"All right." I could see why Gussie was so successful in the union. She had a way of convincin' ye to do things ye feared. I wondered how many poor unsuspectin' girls she had talked into goin' on strike, when all they really wanted to do was stay workin' at their machines so they could bring money home to their families. Ma had always taught me to stay out of trouble. Now here I was brazenly askin' for it.

"Can I go?" Maureen asked.

"No," Gussie said. "We might have to leave quickly, and I don't want you to get hurt."

Maureen's eyes widened. "Hurt? Is Rose goin' to get hurt?"

"Probably not," Gussie said.

I didn't like the sound of that. "*Probably* not?"

"I said we wouldn't be arrested, Rose. We won't give him time for that. But how do I know how he'll react when we get there? I don't know the man."

"I don't need a coat that badly," I said. "And as for the money, I'll get another job."

Gussie put her hands on her hips and gave me a stern look that reminded me of Ma. "I'm sure you will, Rose. And when that boss decides not to pay you, you'll run away and find another job, won't you? There are people running sweatshops all over the Lower East Side who would love to hire a meek little greenhorn like you."

I stood up and faced her, but all I managed to say was, "I'm not meek," in a voice so tremulous that it proved her point, not mine.

Gussie pulled a woolen shawl from the back of her father's chair and wrapped it around my shoulders. "You won't be such a mouse when I get through with you. Now, let's go show that man how tough you can be."

Before I could speak, she had me out the door. She kept her arm around my shoulder, forcin' me to keep goin' as we marched down the sidewalk. I half expected her to be wavin' a union banner in her other hand. My heart was in my throat, but I didn't dare protest. I knew I had to get a good deal stronger if I was to keep Maureen and me off the streets, and, like it or not, Gussie was the perfect teacher. Still, I balked when we got to the building. "I can't! I don't want to see that man again, Gussie. I feel sick to my stomach."

Gussie gave me that look again. "Then go over to the curb, be sick, and get it over with."

I took a deep breath. "No, it's all right. I'll do it. The shop is in the back. We go through here."

I led the way through the hall of the front apartment building, but when we stood outside the door of the shop, my legs went weak. I dropped to my knees and vomited on the ground. This was gettin' to be a habit.

Gussie knelt beside me and held back the lock of hair that had fallen into my face. When I was finished, she helped me to my feet, and gestured for me to wipe a bit of vomit off my chin. "You should kiss the old coot now. Might not be such a pleasant experience for him."

I laughed in spite of myself, and Gussie in one motion rubbed my back and shoved me through the door.

Mr. Moscovitz looked surprised. "What do you want? You have no business in this shop."

"Tell him why you're here," Gussie whispered.

I opened my mouth, but I could feel the bile risin' in my throat.

When Gussie saw my face, she spoke for me. "She does indeed have business with you, Mr. Moscovitz."

I swallowed the bitter liquid in my mouth and shivered. But when I saw the bandage on Mr. Moscovitz's nose, where I had bitten him, I suddenly felt a strength I didn't know I had. I spotted my coat folded up on a chair and went to claim it. "This belongs to me," I said. Then I walked right up to him and held out my hand. "And I'm here for the money ye owe me for the work I did."

Mr. Moscovitz dismissed me with a wave of his hand. "Take your ratty old coat, but I owe you nothing."

"Ye owe me for a day's work I did here in the shop and three thousand stems I made at home."

Mr. Moscovitz jutted out his chin. "I pay nothing for shoddy work."

I was aware that all eyes in the room were on me, but I didn't look at the other girls. The only sound was the soft rustle of paper petals.

Mr. Moscovitz raised his hand as if to cuff me on the side of the face. Instead of shrinkin' back, I stepped forward, almost nose to nose with him. "The lady with me is from the union. She says ye have to pay me."

Mr. Moscovitz stepped back. I couldn't tell if it was from my words or my stinkin' breath. "Nonsense. This isn't a union shop."

I moved in close again. I could see that, even with the early-mornin' chill in the room, he had tiny beads of sweat on his forehead. "It doesn't matter whether ye're a union shop or not. There are laws, y'know. Laws that say ye can't take advantage of yer workers."

The room that had been so silent before now began to sizzle with whispers.

"I can have ye arrested," I said. "Ye know I'm speakin' the

truth. Yer girls know it now, too. I'm sure ye've been cheatin' them as well as me. And maybe been wantin' a few extra favors from some of 'em, too. Especially the young, pretty ones." I glanced over and saw Tessa. She raised her eyebrows at me. The buzz became louder now.

Mr. Moscovitz pushed Gussie and me toward the door. He plunged his hand in his pocket and pulled out some bills. "Take this and leave," he said, thrustin' them into my hand. "I don't ever want to see you again."

"Don't worry, you won't!" I shouted over my shoulder as he slammed the door behind us.

We could hear him yellin' through the closed door: "Girls! Girls! Stop this nonsense and get back to work."

There were some voices shoutin' back at him, but I couldn't make out the words.

Gussie laughed. "You've broken open a hornet's nest for that man. I hope he gets stung plenty." She looked at the bills in my hand. "Three dollars! That's a whole week's pay in some of these places. You turned out to be some fighter, Rose. I couldn't have done better myself."

We ran and laughed all the way home. Maureen came out of our room to greet us when we burst into the apartment. "Are ye all right? Did that awful man hurt ye?"

Gussie laughed. "No. I think I'd say Rose hurt him instead."

"Ye hit him?" Maureen gasped.

I hugged her. "No, silly. I just stood up to him, that's all. It felt good to be doin' the yellin' at someone else instead of takin' it for a change."

"Your sister has real spunk, Maureen. We could use more like her in the union."

"I was only tellin' the truth," I said.

Gussie smiled. "Well, you might have exaggerated just a bit."

"About what?"

"There's no doubt that Mr. Moscovitz should be arrested for what he does, but I'm afraid that won't happen. He was right about not being bound by union rules. He didn't have to pay you a cent."

"Well, then, why did he give me all that money?"

"He wanted to get you out of there quickly, so you wouldn't give his girls any ideas."

"I didn't mean to lie," I said.

"Don't worry about it. Obviously Mr. Moscovitz hasn't paid enough attention to the labor movement to understand his own rights. If one girl stands up to him, you did a good deed. Now I have to get to work. I'll find out about getting you a job."

"Can ye get me a job, too?" Maureen asked. "I'm twelve. That's old enough to work."

"You have to be fourteen to be legal," Gussie said. "Unfortunately, the shop owners hire some girls as young as ten. That's why they hide them in the elevator between floors when the inspectors come."

Maureen's face brightened. "See, Rose? I could work with you and Gussie."

"Oh, no, " Gussie said. "I won't get a job for an underage worker. I don't approve of child labor."

"Neither would Ma," I said. "She wants ye in school, and that's exactly where ye're goin'. I'll earn the money."

"I hate you both!" Maureen went off into our room in a huff.

"Too bad she didn't have a door to slam," I said.

Gussie laughed. "The swish of a curtain just doesn't have the same dramatic effect, does it?" She cut herself a slice of bread and a hunk of cheese, wrapped them in paper, and slipped them into her purse. "You should get Maureen signed up for public school right away, Rose. I can see how that one could get herself in a lot of trouble if she had too much time on her hands."

"Ye're right about that!" I said, surprised that Gussie had sized up Maureen so quickly.

Maureen sulked after Gussie left, refusin' to speak to me. That was fine with me. I could use some thinkin' time. I certainly wasn't about to drag her through the streets to find a school. We could go in the afternoon. I spent the mornin' mendin' the torn sleeve of my dress. Luckily, it was just a ripped seam, so it was an easy fix. Besides, it got my fingers back in the habit of sewin' again.

I wondered what it would be like to work in a big factory. How many girls did Gussie say worked there? Hundreds? I couldn't even imagine it. Still, it would be steady work if I could get it. And the conditions at the Triangle Shirtwaist Factory must be fair and safe, or Gussie wouldn't be workin' there. As soon as I had the job, I planned to write to Ma and tell her how my luck had changed.

21

That night, Gussie came home with a handsome young man who was carryin' a sewin' machine. "This is Jacob Gerstein, a cutter from work. We got this machine from the Jewish settlement house. They said you can keep it for a week."

"I'm . . . I'm grateful to you," I stammered. "I only hope I can learn how to use it in a week. And does it matter that I'm not Jewish?"

Jacob set the machine in the corner of the kitchen. "First, you'll forget about the hoping and just learn quickly. And as for not being Jewish, the machine won't know the difference, unless you make a big thing of it."

His first remark stung, but he was grinnin' when he looked up, and I realized he was makin' a joke.

"I'll work very hard," I said.

Jacob pulled two chairs over to the machine. "Good. Let's get started."

He showed me how to work the treadle with my feet. It stuck at first, until Jacob gave the flywheel on the side of the machine a pull. Then it took off like the horses on a fire wagon. I thought my feet would break off at the ankles from rockin' back and forth on the treadle. "How do I stop it?" I shouted. "It's gettin' away from me."

Jacob laughed. "You're keeping it going with your feet."

As soon as I took my feet off the treadle, the machine stopped. I pushed my chair back. "This thing has a life of its own. Aren't there some jobs at the factory where you just do yer sewin' by hand?"

Maureen, who had been hangin' over my shoulder, tugged at Jacob's sleeve. "Teach me. I'm not afraid. I'll learn faster than Rose."

"Leave him be, Maureen," I said. "Ye're not workin' at any factory." I pulled my chair back to the machine. "All right, Jacob. Teach me more."

Jacob took a scrap of cloth and showed me how to run it under the needle. "You have to watch what you're doing. The machine doesn't know the difference between fabric and fingers and would just as soon stitch you to the bone as make a seam."

I shuddered at that remark, pullin' my hands away as the fabric approached the needle. The scrap suddenly turned to the right, jammin' itself under the needle and breakin' the thread.

Jacob pushed my hands away, straightened out the mess,

and rethreaded the machine. "Now, you want to be cautious, but you need to hold the fabric until it's all the way past the needle. If you had done that at the Triangle, you would have ruined the fabric. It's lawn, very sheer and hard to handle. The machine can tear it to shreds if you're not careful, and that will be taken out of your pay."

"I'm sorry." I blushed, but only partly from embarrassment at my lack of sewin' skills. I wasn't used to bein' this close to a young man. He was leanin' in so far to watch my hands, our cheeks almost touched. This certainly wasn't helpin' me to keep my hands steady. I wondered if Jacob and Gussie were sweet on each other. She was payin' little attention to him, busyin' herself with makin' tea, but I thought her face looked a little rosier than usual, and she did glance over at us several times. There was no need of her to be jealous of me. Jacob was obviously interested only in my fingers and their ability to guide the fabric without gettin' themselves stitched into a mitten.

I began to get the feel of the machine, so it didn't frighten me as much. What small, even stitches it produced! Ma had made me practice sewin' for hours on end, and here was a machine that could do it for me. I felt a pang of homesickness for Ma. Did she miss Maureen and me, or had she already washed her hands of us?

After Jacob was satisfied that I was safe to be left untended, he stood up. "You're getting the idea now. I'll try to nip some scraps of lawn from work tomorrow to let you practice on the real thing."

"You know you'll get in trouble if you get caught," Gussie said.

"They don't check the men as carefully as they do the girls," Jacob said. "Especially the cutters."

Gussie frowned. "That's another thing that makes me angry. We have to open our purses for inspection before they let us out of the building. The men get to waltz right through with Lord knows what in their pockets, and they get paid more in the bargain."

Jacob kissed her on the forehead—a sort of brother-to-sister kiss, I thought. "Ah, always the union activist, Gussie. Don't you ever just relax and enjoy life?"

"I'll relax when things are fair," Gussie snapped.

Just then the door opened and Mr. Garoff came in carryin' a loaf of black bread. Jacob's manner changed right away, and he became serious and proper.

"What's this I have in my kitchen?" Mr. Garoff bellowed. "We're now a sweatshop?"

"I was just teaching your *roomerkeh* to work a machine, sir," Jacob said.

Mr. Garoff slammed the loaf down on the table. "A school I'm running?"

"It's only for a week, Papa," Gussie said. "Rose needs to learn so she can get a job at the Triangle. You want her to be able to pay the rent, don't you?"

Mr. Garoff's bushy eyebrows met in the center of his forehead. "I want? It matters what I want? Well, I want a tenant who has a job and money to pay the rent."

Gussie patted her father on the shoulder and gestured with her head toward the door.

Jacob got the message. He backed quickly toward the exit, tippin' his hat to Mr. Garoff. "I was just leaving, sir. It's a pleasure to see you in such good health, sir. I was just . . ."

Mr. Garoff turned toward him and gave him such a look, Jacob shrank through the door, closin' it quickly behind him.

Mr. Garoff pulled one of the chairs away from the machine and over to the table. "So—this Jacob. He is courting you? No?"

"No, Papa," Gussie said. "I know him from work. I needed someone strong to carry the machine home."

"You need someone strong for a husband. Someone to support you. A man can only take care of his children for so long, then they should take care of themselves."

I saw Gussie bite her lip. I knew she must be supportin' her father instead of the other way around. He didn't seem to have any sort of job. Still, I could tell she didn't want to hurt him. "I'm a long way from marriage, Papa. I have much work to do first."

"Pah! You and your union. The mice in the walls think they own the whole house. The owners of that factory could fire you all tomorrow and hire what comes off the next boat. You fight a battle you cannot win."

Gussie raised her chin and looked her father in the eye. "No, Papa. We fight a battle we cannot lose."

22

By the end of the week, I was confident in runnin' the machine. I had even practiced on some scraps of the sheer fabric that Jacob had smuggled out of the building. Still, when Gussie took me to work with her Monday mornin', I was full of doubt. "What if somethin' goes wrong? What if I jam up the fabric and ruin it before I've earned any money? How will I pay for the damage?"

Gussie shook her head. "You worry too much, Rose. You're starting this job knowing how to use a machine. Some of the girls are complete novices when they begin."

In spite of Gussie's encouragin' words, I dreaded my first day of work. But as we walked along, I noticed that more and more people were comin' out into the streets, walkin' to their jobs. And I imagined that they had all felt scared on their first day. After all, wasn't this why I had wanted to come to America in the first place, so I could make my way on my own instead of bein' taken care of, first by my parents, then by a husband? Would Da and Ma be proud of me if they could see me now?

The sun came out as we reached Washington Square. There was a huge stone arch in the park that reminded me of pictures I'd seen of the great arch in Paris.

Gussie noticed me admirin' it. "It's pretty, isn't it? Wait till you see this place when the trees leaf out. One week from tomorrow will be the first day of spring. When the weather warms up, we can eat our lunch here in the park."

"Are we almost there?" I asked. "Can you see it from here?"

"The Triangle factory is on the top three floors of the Asch Building, down Washington Place, over there. We have to go around to the Greene Street side. They don't allow us to use the front entrance."

Girls were comin' across the park from all directions now, everyone headed for the same place. Most of them seemed to be about Gussie's age. I was surprised to see how elegantly some of them were dressed, with hats as big as upturned washbasins. Some of the hats were adorned with feathers, and a few had silk roses the size of cabbages. I knew New York was the center of fashion, but some of these costumes seemed a bit much to me. They were what Ma would have called highfalutin.

A number of the girls waved to Gussie as we walked along. Three of them fell into step with us. Gussie introduced me as her friend and told me their names were Bertha, Esther, and Dora.

Bertha laughed. "You're dragging this poor young thing to work her hands bloody at the Triangle?"

I must have looked as frightened as I felt, because Dora touched my arm to reassure me. "Don't listen to Bertha. The people here at the Triangle are nice, very nice to work for. We have a good time, and we make the best pay in the needle trades. We're sorry to lose you from the eighth floor, though, Gussie. What's it like to be back among the masses again?"

Gussie's face turned red. "It's fine. Now I'll be able to help Rose through her first few days."

"I've never known you to be late before," Esther said. "We tried to tell Mr. Bernstein not to give away your place, but he brought down a young Italian woman from the ninth. Probably doesn't have to pay her as much as he paid you, what with your experience and all. Did they give you a pay cut to go back on the ninth?"

"It's all right," Gussie said, keepin' her eyes on the sidewalk.

"Well, a pay cut wouldn't be all right with me," Esther said. "After all the time it took me to work up to sample-maker. Why didn't you send in a message with someone? There are several Triangle workers on Sullivan Street. If Mr. Bernstein had known you were coming, he would have waited for you."

"I did send a message," Gussie said. "It just didn't get delivered. What's done is done."

Suddenly I realized they were talkin' about the day Gussie went with me to Moscovitz's shop. I had caused her to lose her job as a sample-maker, and now she had suffered a pay cut because of helpin' me. I felt terrible, but I didn't know what to say, especially in front of the other girls.

Four handsome young men passed us and went on ahead.

"Do they work at the Triangle?" I asked.

Bertha laughed. "Hardly. They're college boys. New York University is in the next building to us, but don't expect you'll be mixing with them. They think they're too good to give us as much as a how-d'ye-do, just because their daddies have enough money to send them to a ritzy school." She purposely had been talking loud enough for them to hear. One of the boys turned around and made a face at us. I'd be sure to avoid them in the future. I wanted nothin' to do with people who thought they were better than me. I'd had enough of that with Uncle Patrick's family.

When we started down Washington Place, I saw the Asch Building. It had signs for clothing companies runnin' all the way up the corner. The highest sign said "Triangle Waist Company." I'd never been in anything so tall.

As we turned the corner onto Greene Street, somethin' glinted in the sunlight and caught my attention. The sidewalk was filled with thick pieces of glass the size of silver dollars. "Will ye look at this? They have little windows in the sidewalk."

"They're called deadlights," Gussie said. "They let light into the basement."

By the time we reached the entrance, we had to take our place in line.

"Why is it movin' so slowly?" I asked.

"The elevators can take only about a dozen people at a time."

Elevators. I'd heard of them, but had never seen one. It didn't seem natural havin' a little room hauled up a cable. As we reached the door, I could feel the crowd pressin' in from behind. "I've never been in an elevator," I said. "Is there a flight of stairs I could climb instead?"

I had been speakin' to Gussie, but a girl on the other side of me answered. "You must be new here. Just be thankful they let us use the elevator in the morning, because they want to get us up to work in a hurry. At night, when we're so tired we can hardly move, they make us walk down."

Another girl looked over her shoulder. "That's a fact. They just want to get their money's worth out of us. More than their money's worth, if you ask me. And don't ever be late. They lock the doors at eight sharp and don't open them again until noon, so you get only half a day's pay."

I was tempted to ask them more about workin' at the Triangle, but I didn't want Gussie to think I was questionin' the job and not grateful for gettin' it. Just then, the elevator doors opened and I was swept inside with the crowd. The elevator operator closed the iron doors with a clang. He pulled the cable, and we suddenly started to rise. My knees gave out from under me, but we were so packed in, there wasn't room for me to fall. I stood in terror as our metal cage moved up the narrow shaft. I felt like a fish being pulled up in a net. When we came to a stop, I was thrown off balance again.

All the men and a few girls got off at the eighth floor. I saw a table of sewin' machines against a wall of windows. The rest of the room had about half a dozen tables with some men already workin' at them, layin' out thick piles of fabric.

The trip from the eighth to the ninth floor was slower. As soon as the doors opened, we were pushed out into the room. I was shocked to see how crowded it was. The entire room was filled with long tables placed close together, with a double row of sewin' machines stretchin' from end to end of each one. Girls were makin' their way down the rows to their places, callin' to each other and wavin'.

"Come," Gussie said. "I'll show you where we put our coats." She led me around a partition to a dressing room where dozens of girls were hangin' up their coats and hats. Some of the feathered hats were so fancy they looked like rare birds.

Gussie poked my arm. "Don't just stand there staring. If you want to use the bathroom, do it now, because you won't be able to after work starts."

I pulled off my coat and hat, still fascinated with all the activity. One girl had taken off her skirt, turned it inside out, and was puttin' it back on. "What's she doin'?" I whispered to Gussie.

"She's turning her skirt so it doesn't get dirty from the machine or get covered with lint and threads. Frankly, I prefer sturdy clothes that will wear like iron, instead of those thin wool suits. Fancy clothes don't hold up well for factory work."

Gussie took my coat and hung it on a hook. "Come on. I'll introduce you to the forelady, and we'll get you set up at a machine."

My heart was beatin' fast, like I had just run a mile. How could I ever do this? All of these girls seemed so sure of themselves. They would walk into that big room and know exactly what to do.

This would be just like Mr. Moscovitz's flower shop, only here, instead of ten pairs of eyes watchin' me, there would be more than two hundred. I could imagine the sound of all those girls laughin' at me. Why had I stayed here instead of goin' home with Ma? I'd be halfway to Limerick by now. Then I'd work in some little shop or maybe even take in sewin' at home. It wouldn't be an adventure, but it would be safe. Grandma always said my bein' headstrong was a curse. Now I knew she was right.

With a hand on my elbow, Gussie had been firmly pushin' me across the room to a woman named Anna Gullo. My mind was racin' so fast I could hardly make sense of my own thoughts, much less what people were sayin' to me. The woman told Gussie to have me sit at the machine next to her. Then Gussie had me by the hand and was leadin' me down one of the aisles between tables. Some of the girls were already at their machines. The tables were so close to each other, it was difficult to squeeze past when two girls were seated back to back. Our spot was about halfway down the aisle, which put us almost in the exact center of the huge room.

There was a shallow trough runnin' down the center of the table for its full length. A large wicker basket to my right was filled with cut pieces of cloth.

"I want to show you as much as I can before they pull the switches," Gussie said.

"What switches?"

"The power that runs the machines. It gets noisy then." Gussie pushed her chair back. "Look under the table. See that long axle running about eight inches off the floor? That's hooked to a motor that makes it spin, and that leather belt looped over the flywheel on each machine is what makes it run."

"Ye mean I don't have to work the treadle with my feet?"

"You only push down on the treadle to connect to the power. Then the machine runs itself. It's much easier than the machine you worked on at home."

"But how do I stop it?"

"Just let up on the treadle. And mind you don't knock into that little wooden shell just over your knees. It holds the oil drippings from the machine." Gussie took some fabric from my basket. "Now, when we start, you're going to line up these two pieces of fabric and stitch the seam."

I took the fabric from her. "What is it?"

161

"It's the back of the waist and one half of the front. You want the straight line of the front going right down the center. Make sure you don't sew them together this way." She took it back and flipped one piece around. "Do you see what I mean?"

"It looks every bit as good as the other way around to me. I can't for the life of me see how this makes a shirtwaist."

"It goes like this. See?" Gussie held the pieces of fabric up to herself and showed me how the round cutout would later meet with the sleeve. Now I could see how my section fit into the whole waist like a puzzle piece.

Suddenly a bell rang. "Here we go," Gussie said. "Get ready."

There was a low rumble that made the floor shudder, followed by a raspy sound from all around me, as if hundreds of bumblebees the size of cats had flown in and settled on the tables. "Saints preserve us," I whispered, grippin' the edge of the table.

Gussie laughed. "You'll get used to it. Like this. Watch." When she pressed on the treadle, her machine sprang to life, and she guided the flimsy cloth past the needle. When she held it up, she had a perfect seam. Then, without cuttin' the threads, she took another set of pieces and sewed them together. Soon she had a whole string of them, and she pushed them into the trough in front of her. "See? It's not hard."

I took a deep breath, lined up my fabric in front of the needle, and pressed on the treadle. The needle started movin' up and down with such speed, I was payin' more attention to it than I was to my own fingers. It wasn't until a spurt of red covered my pieces of fabric that I realized the needle was goin' through my finger.

"Let up on the treadle," Gussie shouted. Her words made no sense until she kicked my foot away and the needle stopped, still plunged deep into my finger.

Gussie held my hand still as she moved the flywheel to lift the needle. It must have stabbed me three times before Gussie disconnected the machine.

"I've ruined the fabric," I said.

"Not to mention what you've done to your finger." She blotted the blood away from the end of my finger with the ruined fabric, then snipped the threads and pulled the stitches out of my flesh. For the first time my mind connected with the pain I hadn't felt before. My finger throbbed as Gussie pressed the fabric against my wound. "Lucky the needle didn't go through your fingernail. That's excruciating when it swells up." She dabbed away the blood. "This is just through your fingertip. It should heal up fast. Here comes Mary Leventhal with the first-aid kit. She'll have you fixed up in no time."

A pretty, blond woman came down the aisle, opened up a small box, and took out some supplies. Then she dabbed my finger with iodine and bandaged it tightly.

"I'm sorry," I said. "I feel so stupid."

Mary smiled. "Don't worry. This happens to everyone sooner or later. I must say, you're the soonest we've ever had, though. Now, make sure your finger has stopped bleeding before you start in again."

I wanted to tell her I wasn't ever startin' in again. I wanted to run out of the room and keep runnin'. But I just watched her slowly zigzag her way down our row, swivelin' her slender hips to squeeze past the chairs and the wicker baskets on the floor. I looked around the huge room. There was a sea of machines, and each one had a young girl bent over it. Had they all been as clumsy as me at one time? Had they all sat with a bandaged finger feelin' like a fool?

Gussie patted my shoulder. "Are you all right?"

"This is too hard, Gussie," I whispered. "I'll never learn how to do it right."

"Don't be silly. They say you learn best from your mistakes. At this rate, you should be a very fast learner."

The girls across from us smiled at Gussie's remark, but nobody laughed. Not one single person.

23

When *Mr. Garoff saw* my bandaged finger that night, he started arguin' with Gussie in Yiddish. I had begun to learn some Yiddish words, but they were speakin' so fast, I couldn't understand. I knew the discussion was about me, but I couldn't tell if Mr. Garoff was upset because I had been hurt or because I had been stupid and clumsy. Either way, I wasn't about to listen. I slipped past them into our room. But then I had to endure Maureen's endless questions about my first day of work and how I had been injured. She made a face when I described how the needle had gone through my finger over and over. "Ye still want to work in a factory, Maureen?"

"Of course I do. And I wouldn't be so foolish as to sew up my finger, either. Why didn't ye pull away the first time the needle stabbed ye?"

I couldn't explain why I hadn't pulled away, or why I

hadn't even felt the pain. "Ye don't know what it's like. Things aren't as simple as ye think."

Maureen plunked herself down on the feather bed. "Well, all I know is I'm not learnin' anything in school and I might as well be earnin' some money."

"Why aren't ye learnin'?"

"Because most of the other children don't speak English. The teacher spends the whole time tryin' to learn them the English words."

"Tryin' to *teach* them the English words."

"That's what I said."

"No, ye said 'learn them.' That's not correct, and it makes ye sound stupid. That's why ye need to stay in school."

Maureen studied me for a minute. "Well, maybe I don't always get the words right, but I'm not stupid enough to stab myself with a needle. Three times, for the love of heaven!"

I didn't give Maureen the satisfaction of a response, but that didn't stop her. "There's another thing I don't like. The teacher goes on and on about how we have to wash ourselves—she calls it 'hygiene'—and how we have to have good manners."

"Doesn't sound like either of those things is goin' to hurt ye, especially the manners part."

"I'm tired of it," Maureen whined. "All she talks about is how she's goin' to make us all into Americans."

I grabbed her by the shoulders and pulled her to her feet. "There are hundreds of girls in Ireland who would give their right hands to be made into Americans. And ye're gettin' a good education that's free for the takin'. If I hear any more complainin' from ye, I'm goin' to use my first paycheck to ship ye back home. I don't know why I agreed to let ye stay in the first place. Ye've been nothin' but trouble since the day we saw Ma and Bridget off at the docks."

Maureen gave me a murderous look, but she didn't say anything more.

My sister and I weren't gettin' along, but things were goin' better at the Triangle. Once I got used to the machine, I almost enjoyed the work. I couldn't get over my fear of the elevator, though. It just didn't seem natural to be crowded into that little cage. I climbed the stairs the second day of work. I took them two at a time so I wouldn't be late.

I was lookin' forward to lunch, but when the bell rang, Gussie told me she had some union business to take care of. "You don't mind, do you, Rose? We're having a meeting next week, and I want to tell some of the new girls about it."

"Don't worry about me," I said, but I didn't relish the thought of eatin' alone. I had noticed that some of the girls ate right at their machines, so I decided to do the same. I pulled out my little package of bread and cheese and began to unwrap the paper.

The girls across from me had started down the aisle when one of them came back. "Come have lunch with us. If you eat at your machine, you won't even feel as if you've had a break."

"Thank ye," I said, and followed them to the far corner of the room, where we sat on some boxes. They were dressed alike, in the dark skirts and Gibson Girl shirtwaists favored by most of the Triangle workers. They were about the same size and coloring, too, but one had long hair that fell into shiny black ringlets, the other a wild mane of dark hair that she had tried to tame by twistin' it in a bun and pinnin' it on top of her head.

"I'm Rose Bellini," the one with ringlets said. "What's your name?"

"Now, isn't that a coincidence. I'm Rose, too. Rose Nolan."

They both laughed. "Well, that's something," the other girl said. "I'm another Rose. Rose Klein. So I guess you'll fit in here just fine, Rose Nolan."

We had a wonderful lunch. Rose Bellini was a little on the quiet side, probably because Rose Klein didn't hardly let her get a word in. Rose Klein seemed to know everything that was going on in New York and told me more about herself in twenty minutes than I'd learned about my own self in my whole lifetime. She had three boyfriends, and none of them knew about the others. One of them wasn't even Jewish, which she said her father would kill her for if he found out. I knew I should be shocked by all this. Rose Klein was exactly the kind of girl Ma would tell me to avoid, but there was somethin' about her laugh and the mischievous sparkle in her eyes that made me want to hear more of her scandalous tales.

"So what about you, Rose Nolan?" she asked. "Have you broken any hearts lately?"

I could feel myself blushin'. "Oh, no. I don't even know any boys in America."

Rose Klein winked. "Well, we'll have to change that, won't we? I'm working on finding a beau for Rose, too. Rose Bellini, that is." She leaned back and pinned up a stray lock of hair. "This is too confusing, with three Roses. Why don't we just go by our last names? Klein, Nolan, and Bellini."

"Makes us sound like a vaudeville act," Bellini offered, and we all laughed.

Klein leaned forward. "Bellini here could be on the vaudeville stage if she wanted to. She sings like an angel."

Bellini blushed. "Oh, Rose, you know my family would disown me if I ever tried such a thing."

Klein shook her head. "It's a great waste. By the way, the name's Klein."

Bellini giggled. "Sorry. I forgot."

The afternoon went much faster, now that I had a couple of friends sittin' right across from me. And I wouldn't have to be so dependent on Gussie. She was a nice person and all, but I was glad to have some chums who weren't so serious all the time.

I could hardly wait to get to work the next mornin' to hear all the gossip and jokin' in the dressin' room. Klein convinced Bellini to sing a new song, "Every Little Movement

Has a Meaning All Its Own." Her voice was clear as a bell. We had a lot of singers in our family back home, but I'd never heard the likes of her before. Everybody cheered when she finished.

When I got to my machine, Gussie was already there, threadin' her needle. "I thought you got lost."

"I was just in the dressing room. You should have heard Bellini sing."

"Who?"

"Rose Bellini. She and Rose Klein and I all call each other by our last names, on account of us all bein' named Rose. Here they come now."

"They don't pay you to be singing and fooling around," Gussie said, not lookin' up.

Klein heard Gussie's remark and made a face, then winked. I didn't want to be disloyal to Gussie, but I did wish she'd loosen up once in a while.

That day at lunch, Klein was talkin' about the latest book she had read. "How about you, Nolan?" she asked. "Have you read any good dime novels lately?"

"I don't know what a dime novel is," I said.

Klein put her hands on her hips. "Knock me down and call me dead! You mean to tell me you've never read a dime novel?"

I shook my head.

"Well, I guess you can be excused, because you're new in the country. Wait here." She ran over to the dressin' room and came back with a small paperback book. "You may take this home with you, but I want it back. I'm collecting these."

"Oh, *The Heiress of Cameron Hill*," Bellini said. "That's a good one. Helena, the heroine, is a working girl just like us. She's so brave. Right in the very beginning of the book she's been laid off, so she—"

Klein interrupted her. "Don't tell her the whole story. You'll take all the suspense out of it."

I thumbed through the pages of the book. I'd never had a book that I could take home to read just for the fun of it. "I'll take good care of it," I said, slippin' it into my purse.

"You know what we should do this weekend?" Klein said. "We should go to the nickelodeon, just the three of us. We could go right after work on Saturday."

"Oh, let's do," Bellini said. "*The Lonedale Operator* is playing at the Strand. That's about a working girl, too. She's a telegraph operator. I've been wanting to see it."

Klein looked at me. "What do you say, Nolan? You have been to the nickelodeon, haven't you? Surely the movies have reached Ireland."

"I've never seen one," I admitted, "but I'd love to go. Of course, I'll have to check to see if it's all right."

"Check with who?" Bellini asked. "You have no parents here, do you?"

"There's my younger sister. I have to keep track of her when I'm not workin'. She's been givin' me some trouble lately."

"Have her meet you here when work is out," Klein said. "She can come with us."

"Well," I said, "I'm sure she'd enjoy it, but I don't know if I should spend the money."

Klein folded up her lunch bag and brushed the crumbs from her skirt. "Nonsense. You work hard for your pay. You should get to enjoy some of it. After all, you only live once, Nolan, and life is short at that. You could be run down by a horse cart tomorrow and die never having seen a movie." She grinned. "Now, that would be a real tragedy."

"All right," I said. "I guess it's high time I started to enjoy myself." I thought maybe Maureen would be less of a problem if she started havin' some fun, too.

When I got back to my machine, I felt a warm glow. I was excited about my new life, and I finally had somethin' to write to Ma about. For the first time, I was somebody. I was Rose Nolan, American workin' girl.

24

At the end of the day, I waited for Gussie in the dressing room. She was busy talkin' to some of the girls. I didn't have to hear her to know she was tryin' to convince them to join the union. She kept slappin' her right index finger on her left palm to emphasize the points she was makin'. I was surprised that she looked so much older than the other girls, because I knew she was only eighteen. Gussie could be called pretty, but she was always so earnest, she had made a permanent crease between her brows, addin' ten years to her face.

I knew Gussie had little interest in what she called frivolous things, but it wouldn't hurt her to spend more time on her appearance. With a little effort, her wonderful thick brown hair could be coaxed into a modern style. I wanted to try the new Gibson Girl hairdo that many of the girls wore, with the hair all puffed out on the sides and gathered into a bun at the top of the head. Maybe Gussie and I could help each other try new hairdos at home. That way I wouldn't have to say anything about how her style was unbecomin' and hurt her feelings. And maybe I could convince her to go out to the nickelodeon with us. I'd soften up Gussie yet. She deserved fun as much as the next girl.

Klein came over to me. "So you've survived your first three days at the Triangle, Nolan. How does it feel to be earning a living?"

"It's wonderful. I had no idea workin' could be so much fun."

"It'll be even more fun when you get your first pay envelope." She buttoned up the bright-red coat that cinched in to show off her tiny waist. Her hat was adorned with at least half a dozen matchin' red roses. She noticed me lookin' at the hat. "You like it?" She twirled around so I could see it from all sides. "The hat was perfectly plain when I got it. Then I bought the roses from a cart on Hester Street for ten cents."

"It's nice," I said. "I guess I should get somethin' more fashionable."

She looked at the shapeless wool cap I wore and winked. "I was going to suggest that. We'll go shopping together after you get paid a week from Saturday. I know how to make your money go a long way. Let's get out of this place."

"I have to wait for Gussie."

Klein wrinkled her nose. "She can get home by herself. Besides, I don't want to walk with her. I've almost saved up enough to buy new shoes with French heels, but she'll want me to give it up for union dues. Come on."

It didn't seem right to leave Gussie behind, since she was the one who got me the job and all. But then I decided Gussie had business to attend to and probably wouldn't even miss me.

Bellini joined us as we headed for the stairs. When we got outside, the three of us walked arm in arm toward Washington Square. They were singin' some new song at the top of their lungs. When I didn't know the words, they switched to "My Wild Irish Rose."

"Surely you know this one," Klein said. I did, even though it was an American song rather than an Irish one. It had made its way across the ocean and was bein' sung in Limerick before we left. I joined in with gusto. We followed the semicircular sidewalk that cut off the corner of the park. When we got to West Broadway and Washington Square South, Bellini unlinked arms with me. "Here's where I leave you. See you tomorrow." She skipped backward a few steps and waved to us before runnin' to catch up with a large group of girls headin' west.

"Where does she live?" I asked.

"On Grove Street in the West Village. Lots of the Italian girls live around there. Where are you heading, by the way?"

"I'm on Sullivan Street, near Broome."

Klein smiled. "We're practically neighbors. I'm on Spring. Want to walk together in the morning?"

"I guess I should go in with Gussie," I said. "We leave the apartment at the same time."

"Ah, yes," Klein said. "We don't want to cross Gussie, do we?"

I thought she was serious, but then she laughed and launched into the plot of the movie she'd seen at the nickelodeon the week before. What a story! A young workin' girl who had so many misfortunes, ye thought she'd never survive, but she managed to triumph in the end and marry the rich factory-owner. I was so caught up in the story, the blocks fairly flew by until Klein said, "Here's where I say goodbye, unless you're coming home with me. You're welcome to do that, but my mother is a *noodge*. She'll drive you mad."

"My mother can be a *noodge* at times, too," I said, and Klein laughed at hearin' me use a Yiddish word.

I got thinkin' about Ma on the way home. Klein and Bellini both lived with their families. How perfect it would be to have Ma and Da here. I could come home every day bubblin' over with stories from work. And Da would have some political job and go around in a nice suit and hat like Uncle Patrick, instead of wearin' the ratty old clothes he wore when he delivered coal. When I was younger, Da sometimes let me ride along with him on his coal route. Even when we went across Sarsfield Bridge to some of the big houses off the Ennis Road, I could tell that Da's customers liked him. He could be covered with coal dust from head to foot, but people treated him with respect. Da had a way with people. He'd make a good politician—as good as Uncle Patrick. Ma could dress up and go visitin' like Elsa, then make fancy dresses at home. I looked at some of the buildings along the way, tryin' to picture what it would be like to live in one of them with my whole family and have a real home again.

Maureen was in her usual grumpy mood when I got back to the apartment, but today I had a way to cheer her up. "Ye'll never guess where we're going Saturday, after I get out of work," I said. This got her interest, and she forgot to stick out her lower lip.

"Where?"

"To the nickelodeon."

"Really? Oh, Rose, do ye mean it?"

It seemed good to see Maureen smile for a change. "I surely do. But I don't want to hear any complaints about school for the rest of the week, is that clear? And I want ye to work hard at your studies." I put my purse on the table and sat down.

"Oh, I will, Rose! I will."

"I'm goin' to write to Ma now, so leave me be."

"Maybe ye should wait till after we go to the nickelodeon. Ma would like to hear about that."

Just then the door opened and Gussie came in. "I looked all over for you. Where did you go?"

"I'm sorry," I said. "Ye were busy talkin' to people, so I left."

Gussie took off her coat and hung it on a hook. "That's fine, but next time let me know you're leaving. I wasn't sure you knew the way home."

Maureen was fairly burstin'. She grabbed Gussie's hands and spun her around. "Gussie, Rose says we're goin' to the nickelodeon on Saturday." Then she stopped and looked down. "What's that funny noise yer shoes are makin'?"

Gussie sat down and crossed her legs to show Maureen her shoe. "My heel was broken and I got it repaired. The cobbler put in a steel plate. See? It should last forever, and it only cost five cents. The same price as your nickelodeon."

Maureen wrinkled her nose. "It may last forever, but it's ugly. Besides, it makes ye clump. I'd rather spend my five cents on the nickelodeon any day."

Gussie rolled her eyes. "It must run in the family." She looked over Maureen's head at me. "You do know we have to work on Saturday, don't you?"

"Yes. We're goin' after work. Maureen will come over and meet us."

Gussie raised her eyebrows. "Us?"

"Rose Klein and Rose Bellini and me. Well . . . and you, too, Gussie. I was plannin' to ask ye first thing."

Gussie poured hot water from the kettle into the teapot. "You needn't include me in your plans. I don't have time for nickelodeons. You shouldn't be wasting your money on that nonsense, either. Or on this." She pointed to the copy of *The Heiress of Cameron Hill* that was stickin' out of my purse.

"I didn't buy that. Rose Klein lent it to me."

"Rose Klein doesn't have the good sense God gave her." Gussie went over to a makeshift shelf and pulled out a heavy book. "If you want something worthwhile to read, try this." She plunked a heavy leather-bound copy of *Women in Industry* on the table in front of me.

I flipped through the first few pages. "Ye'll have to forgive me, Gussie, but this doesn't have the same appeal to me."

Gussie folded her arms. "It might be a bit dry, but if you want to learn about working women, you can put up with it."

I held up my dime novel. "But this is about a workin' girl, too. And they make it exciting by puttin' it in the form of a story."

"That's nothing but a fairy tale. The poor girl wins the rich hero in the end, and only because it turns out she's been an heiress all along and didn't know it."

"Ah, so ye read it, did ye?"

"I didn't have to read it," Gussie said. "They're all alike. They just change the name of the girl and what kind of work she does. And it makes it sound like the only thing young girls think about is love and romance."

Hearin' those words, Maureen slipped the book out of my purse and took it into our room. I didn't reprimand her. At least it might keep her out of our hair for a bit. There were things I wanted to say to Gussie, and I didn't need Maureen puttin' in her two cents' worth.

"Well, thanks for spoilin' the whole story for me," I said. "Don't ye ever do anything just for fun, Gussie? Would it kill ye to laugh once in a while?"

Gussie sighed, soundin' for all the world like Ma. "I'd like to have time for fun, Rose, but there's too much work to be done."

"Work is over for today. What's the use of earnin' money if you don't ever take time to enjoy yerself?"

"I'm not talking about work at the Triangle. I want to make conditions better for everybody, no matter where they work."

"Aw, Gussie. Why is it always the blasted union? Yer mind is like an engine that only runs on one track."

Gussie leaned on the table, puttin' her at eye level with me. "You want to know why I care so much about the union, Rose? It's because of Papa. When he came to this country just eight years ago, he was strong and bright, a fine tailor. But, as skilled as he was, he couldn't make much money in Russia. He wanted better for our family. We all heard about how good things were in America."

"Where does he work now?" I asked. I'd never seen any evidence that Mr. Garoff had a job.

"He worked at various places in the needle trades, mostly small sweatshops. They were cold and damp in the winter, stifling hot in the summer, all with poor light. He finally scraped together enough money to send for me. I was the oldest, so I could earn money to help bring Mama and my sisters over. But by the time I got here, Papa's eyesight had failed so much, he couldn't see the stitches anymore. Then he tried to be a presser, but he didn't have the stamina to lift the heavy iron all day. He was out sick so often, he kept losing jobs."

"That's awful," I said. "I had no idea."

Gussie sank heavily into a chair. "Papa is a proud man. He still tries to get jobs, but nobody will hire him anymore. He can't admit even to himself that I'm supporting him instead of the other way around. I'm saving up to bring the family over, but with only me working, it's taking a long time."

"I'm sorry," I said, "but things aren't that bad at the Triangle. It's a nice place to work."

"The Triangle owners don't recognize the union. When they have us work overtime, they don't give us extra pay. They just give everyone a piece of pie for supper, and we're supposed to be grateful. Do you know what they did while we were out on strike? They brought in music and had dance contests during the lunch break for the scab workers. The foolish girls thought they were being treated well. Those dance contests stopped right away when the regular workers came back. Then everything went on as if the strike never had happened."

"Well, I suppose it isn't right, but I have no complaints. And I know it's crowded and all, but I have all the space I need."

Gussie slapped the table. "Rose, wake up! They're cheating us. The law says there has to be two hundred and fifty cubic feet of space for each worker. The Triangle gets around that because of the high ceilings. They have the right number of cubic feet for each of us, but it's all above our heads. What good is that? We're jammed in hip to hip at the floor level. You may not mind it now, but wait till you see how it feels in the heat of July."

Gussie was probably right, but I didn't care if the company was cheatin' us on space. I liked workin' close to my friends so we could glance up and smile at each other every now and then. It felt cozy to me, not cramped. I wished I could get Gussie to loosen up a bit. It was a terrible waste for someone so young to be so serious.

Even though I felt a little guilty, I was glad Gussie wasn't goin' to the nickelodeon with us. She'd probably tell us how the movie ended and spoil the whole thing.

25

🌹 *Goin' to the nickelodeon* turned out to be much more than just watchin' a movie. The show outside the theater was almost as exciting as the one within. There was a large crowd millin' around on the sidewalk, lookin' at the movie posters and talkin'. There were lots of girls I recognized from the Triangle, and a number of young men, too. We hadn't been there more than three minutes before Klein was carryin' on a conversation with two of the handsomest young men. I wondered if they were two of her beaux, findin' out about each other for the first time. But when I asked Bellini about them, she said she'd never seen either of the men before. "It's fine to talk to these boys," she said, "but don't let any of them treat you."

"What do ye mean?"

"A boy might ask to pay your way into the theater, but

then he might think that he had paid for taking certain favors with you. Klein and I always buy our own tickets. That way we're not beholden to anybody."

I didn't ask what Bellini meant by "certain favors," but I had a pretty fair idea since the incident with Moscovitz. I marveled at how Klein did just enough flirtin' to keep both boys interested. I wondered if they were thinkin' one of them might get to treat her. I envied Klein's ease with boys. I was so awkward whenever I was with one, I got all tongue-tied and couldn't keep my face from turnin' red.

I was surprised to hear a man's voice callin' my name, although, with so many girls at the Triangle named Rose, he could have been callin' anybody. I turned to see Jacob, my sewin'-machine teacher, comin' toward me. "Rose. It's good to see you. How have you been?"

"Fine," I said, then fell silent, unable to think of anything else to say.

"Is the work going well for you at the Triangle?"

"Yes." Another silence. What *was* the matter with me? I looked over at Klein, whose mouth hadn't stopped movin' since we arrived at the theater. What on earth could she think to talk about?

"So it helped you to learn the machine before you started work?" Jacob asked.

"Yes." My mind raced to find somethin' to say, but my panic only served to make me mute.

"I'm so glad to run into you," Jacob said, lookin' truly interested.

184

I blushed and smiled. What wonderful entertainment I turned out to be. Surely he must be fascinated with this dolt who could only come up with one-word answers to his questions.

"So—I don't see Gussie. She did come with you, didn't she? I mean, you're new here. You wouldn't have come alone."

"Oh, no," I managed to stammer. "I came with two of my friends from work. Rose Bellini and Rose Klein."

Jacob's eyes searched the crowd over my shoulder. "And Gussie? She isn't here?"

"No. I think she said somethin' about goin' to the union hall."

Jacob smiled and tipped his hat. "Ah, yes. That sounds more like Gussie than the nickelodeon. Good day, Rose. It was nice to see you again." With that, he moved swiftly into the crowd and disappeared. So he hadn't really cared about talkin' to me at all. He simply wanted to see Gussie and had hoped that she was here with me.

I felt a tug at my sleeve. It was Maureen. I had forgotten she had come along with us. "I was lookin' at the posters, Rose. Will the pictures really move?"

"I expect so. Otherwise they wouldn't call them movin' pictures, would they?"

"But how, Rose? How can a picture move?"

"Hush, Maureen. We'll know when we see it. Come along. Bellini and Klein are headin' for the ticket window."

Maureen couldn't stop talkin' all the way into the darkened theater. "You'll have to be quiet when the movie starts," Bellini told her. "If you're noisy, the ushers will make you leave."

We took our places in a row near the front. Klein went in first, then Bellini, followed by me, with Maureen on the aisle. I noticed the two young men who had been talkin' to Klein slipped into the row behind us.

The theater was hummin' with conversation, but when the lights dimmed, there was a hush. Then there was a clackety sound and a flickerin' light appeared on the screen forming the words *The Lonedale Operator*. A piano player down front by the screen started a lively tune. The letters jiggled a little on the screen, but it didn't seem much different from my Grandma Nolan's magic lantern when somebody bumped the table it was sittin' on.

Then it happened. A woman's picture appeared, but this was no magic-lantern picture. She moved—really moved. She waved her arms around, then stood up. I let out a squeal—I couldn't help it—and started to giggle.

Bellini poked me. "Nolan, be quiet."

I couldn't stop laughin'. It was the most amazin' thing I had ever seen. A man walked into the picture. He and the woman seemed to be talkin' to each other.

Klein leaned over Bellini. "Nolan, what's the matter with you?"

I couldn't answer. I couldn't even catch my breath. Now Maureen had picked up my case of giggles. Suddenly I saw a flashlight out of the corner of my eye. An usher stood at Maureen's elbow. "You are making a disturbance," he whispered.

This struck me funny. It was like the time back in school in Limerick when I was reprimanded by Sister Mary Michael. The madder she got, the sillier I got. It was the first time that I was sent down to Father Monahan's office. It was also the last time, because when Ma heard what I had done I got the lickin' of my life.

The usher reached over and touched my shoulder. "Miss, I'll have to ask you to leave the theater."

Klein leaned forward. "Oh, please, sir. She's just never seen a movie before, and she's taken with the excitement of it. She'll be quiet." Klein gave him her most charmin' smile, and though it was hard to see in the dark, it seemed to have worked.

The usher just said, "Well, all right," and left.

I pressed my fist to my lips to make sure I didn't utter a sound.

The movie was astonishing. It took me a while to realize that the words people were speakin' were written across the screen every few minutes. Soon I became so engrossed in the story, I hadn't a thought of laughin'. I agonized as Mary, the telegraph operator, put herself in great jeopardy to capture a band of train robbers. When the lights went on at the end of the movie, I was breathless. Maureen unfortunately had plenty of breath left to chatter all the way home.

Mr. Garoff was sittin' at the table when we went into the

apartment. "Now you work until nine o'clock at night? Where is Gussela?"

"We weren't workin' all this time, sir," I said.

Maureen slipped into the chair next to him. "We went to the nickelodeon, Mr. Garoff. It was wonderful."

Mr. Garoff jutted out his chin. "You waste your time and money on such nonsense? My Gussela wasn't there, was she?"

"No," I said. "She had some business at the union hall."

"Bad enough my daughter works on Shabbes. Then she works for the union afterward?"

"But we all have to work on Saturday, Mr. Garoff," I said. "Gussie has no choice."

"She has choice. Never has she worked on Shabbes before. She was always home by sundown on Friday night and didn't go back until Monday."

I hadn't known that. Had Gussie's move to the ninth floor meant she had to work an extra day?

It wasn't long before we heard footsteps on the stairs. Gussie came through the door, shakin' the snow from her scarf.

"You have a good reason for working on Shabbes?" her father roared.

"Did you forget, Papa? I don't make as much money now. I have to make up for the cut in pay by working the extra day."

"Not enough that you disgrace yourself by working on Shabbes, you go work for the union after that?"

Gussie took off her coat slowly. "I'm sorry, Papa. It hurts me to offend you. But as for the union work, that was after sundown. No longer Shabbes."

"You do not correct your father," he bellowed. "You bring these *shiksas* into our home and now you act like them. Why did you not go to their foolish nickelodeon? You have become like them, no?"

I watched Maureen's face. Just moments before, she had looked happier than I'd seen her in weeks. Now the smile had faded away, and tears were fillin' her eyes. She started to stand up, but Gussie moved behind her, puttin' her hands on Maureen's shoulders. "Maureen and Rose have done nothing to deserve your anger, Papa. Their beliefs differ from ours, but they are good people."

I couldn't believe Gussie was standin' up for us. I knew she didn't approve of us goin' to the nickelodeon. I knew she was less than fond of my friends, especially Klein. Now she was talkin' back to her father in our defense. I learned somethin' new about Gussie almost every day, but I couldn't begin to understand her.

26

I *finished* readin' *The Heiress of Cameron Hill* over the weekend. Maureen coaxed me into readin' it aloud so she could enjoy it, too. I knew she was a bit young to be learnin' about matters of the heart, but it kept her happy, and that made life much easier for me. Takin' care of Maureen made me appreciate Ma more than I ever had before. She had managed to keep four children in line, not just one. Maureen and I had been gettin' along much better since I had taken her to the nickelodeon. For the first time, I was almost glad I had let her stay with me. It was nice to have some family with me here in America. I didn't count Uncle Patrick's family. Wouldn't they be surprised to find out that we had stayed in this country and were doin' just fine.

The weather was a bit warmer Sunday mornin', so Maureen and I took a walk after Mass to look in the shop windows and laugh at the ridiculous hats. Then we picked out the outfits we would buy if we had some money, right down to the shoes and purse. I was glad Gussie hadn't come along. She would have complained about how these clothes were only cheap copies of the outfits the rich ladies wore, and not suitable for Women of Industry. I had as much fun with Maureen and her sense of humor as I would have had with Klein and Bellini.

We walked along laughin' and talkin' and eventually reached the East River. "I think that's Brooklyn on the other side," I said. "Some of the girls from work live over there."

Maureen shaded her eyes from the sun. "The East River isn't as pretty as the Shannon, d'ye think?"

"I don't know. It's different. Bigger and busier."

"Well, I can't see what good it is to have a river if ye can't swim in it."

I laughed. "And since when do ye go swimmin' on the nineteenth of March?"

"Ye know what I mean," Maureen said. "Where would ye swim here even in the middle of summer? It's not so nice as the Fairy Steps or the Girls Sandy."

I did know what she meant. There were three swimmin' places on the Shannon just up from Thomond Bridge. The Fairy Steps were for the little children and their mothers, with small steps carved into the bank makin' it easy to get to the water. Girls Sandy and Boys Sandy were wider coves for those of us who knew how to swim. Since none of us had proper bathin' attire, the priests warned against swimmin' with the opposite sex. That's why we had the separate places.

But Boys Sandy had a swingin' rope hangin' from a tree limb, and Girls Sandy didn't, because it wasn't ladylike or some such nonsense. So, every now and then when Boys Sandy was empty, I'd have my girl chums keep watch while I jumped for that swingin' rope.

I'd climb the bank, bend my knees, and leap out over the water, arms and legs outstretched. Then I'd grab the rope and wrap my legs around it, swingin' a dozen times before I dropped into the water. It was the closest thing a person could get to flyin'.

The other girls were afraid to do it, except for Maureen. Even when she was much too little, she'd leap off the bank and miss the rope. I must have hauled her drippin' out of the Shannon for five years straight before she finally got it right. Then there was no stoppin' her.

"What are ye thinkin' about, Rose?" Maureen's voice brought me out of my daydream. She grinned at me. "The swingin' rope at Boys Sandy, right?"

"Right," I said, and tousled her hair.

When we got back to our room, I finally wrote a letter home.

19 March 1911

Dear Ma and Da,

I was going to write sooner, but things have turned out different than we expected. Please don't be angry,

192

but we didn't go back to Uncle Patrick's. I know I promised, Ma, but you know how it was to live there, so I think you'll understand.

Don't worry about us, because we are doing just fine. We are renting a room from a nice man and his daughter Gussie. I work with her at a wonderful place called the Triangle Waist Company. We make those fancy Gibson Girl blouses you see in the magazines. I have even learned how to use a sewing machine, can you imagine?

Yesterday we went to see the nickelodeon. I can't wait to show you when you come back. The pictures really move. You would think the people were alive except for them being in black and white.

We're going to Mass every Sunday and Maureen is in school. We miss you and think of you every day. Come back soon.

Love,
Rose

P.S. I hope Bridget is well and Joseph's eyes have cleared up.

Maureen wanted to read the letter before I mailed it, which was a good thing, because I had forgotten to mention Bridget and Joseph. I had also left out Mr. Garoff's name, but that was on purpose. After the fuss Ma made about Elsa bein' Lutheran, I didn't think she'd be any too pleased about us livin' in a Jewish home.

When I went to work on Monday mornin', Maureen headed off for school without the usual argument. My life was settlin' down at last.

I returned the book to Klein at lunchtime, and she gave me another, *The Romance of a Beautiful New York Working Girl*. Bellini couldn't wait to tell me about the movie she wanted to see the next weekend.

"I don't know," I said. "I mean, it was wonderful and I loved every minute of it, but I don't think I should spend the money two weekends in a row."

Klein gave me a section of the orange she had just peeled. "Oh, Nolan, it's only a nickel. Give yourself a little treat. You've been listening to Gussie too much."

"All right. If I don't go, I'll think about it all weekend. I'm afraid I'll have to bring Maureen again, though. She'll have a fit if I go without her."

Thinkin' about the nickelodeon gave me somethin' to look forward to.

The week went by quickly. I loved bein' with my friends, and I had met even more of the girls through Klein and Bellini. We all had a grand time at lunch. One of the male machinists called us "a beautiful bunch of Roses." One day we counted all the girls at the Triangle named Rose. Klein made a list and came up with seventeen. And to think I had changed my given name to sound more unusual. I must have picked the most common name in America.

* * *

I was hummin' to myself Wednesday mornin' as I worked. It all seemed so natural now. My fingers knew how to guide the fabric through the machine without getting stabbed. My right foot knew just exactly how hard to press on the pedal to get the machine to start without lurchin' ahead, and when to let up the pressure so it stopped stitchin' at the exact end of the seam. A steady stream of fabric flowed out of the back of my machine and into the trough at the center of the table.

I looked around the room. Over two hundred girls sat at their machines, rockin' gently forward and back with the rhythm of their work. It was like bein' part of a huge ballet, and I was every bit as graceful as the other dancers. But suddenly I saw somethin' that made me stop my machine in the middle of a seam.

Gussie looked up. "What's wrong?"

I pointed at a small group of young girls who had come into the room. "Look! There's Maureen. What's she doin' here?"

"That man she's with is a subcontractor," Gussie said. "He finds girls who are willing to work for less money and sells their services to the company. Of course, he takes a cut for himself."

I stood up, jammin' the back of my chair into the girl behind me. "Well, if I have anything to say about it, she's goin' to get herself back in school in a hurry." I nearly tripped over my wicker basket in my haste to get to Maureen.

195

As I squeezed behind Gussie, she turned and caught my arm. "Leave her alone, Rose. Don't make a scene."

"Oh, I see, Miss Queen of the Union, it's fine for you to go flappin' yer mouth about how workers get cheated by the bosses, but I can't stop my own sister from bein' a fool?"

Gussie kept her grip on my arm and stood so she could speak quietly into my ear over the noise of the machines. "Of course you'll make her quit and go back to school, but do it tonight, not now. You know how headstrong Maureen is. Do you really want to drag her out of here kicking and screaming and give up a day's wages to get her to school? And do you think your job would be waiting for you when you got back?"

I saw Mary Leventhal lookin' at me from across the room. Gussie was right. I'd make a scene and be fired for sure. But when I got my hands on that little brat back home, I was goin' to wring her neck. And I vowed right that very minute never to have any children—ever! A mother needed the patience of a saint, and I'd never seen sainthood in my future.

I didn't know where they had Maureen workin' that mornin', and Gussie kept me from lookin' for her at the lunch break. "Wait till tonight. Papa will be out visiting his friends from the temple, and I'll be at the union hall, so you'll have the place to yourselves. It will be easier for you to show Maureen who's boss in the privacy of home."

"I'll show her who's boss, all right," I said.

Maureen knew enough to hightail it out of there at the

quittin' bell, so I didn't see her until I got home. I wasted no time gettin' into it with her. "What exactly did ye think ye were doin' today?"

"What d'ye think I was doin'? Workin', of course."

"And just how did ye meet that man?"

"He was at the end of our block by the deli. He asked me if I wanted a job."

"The deli isn't on the way to school."

"Who said I was on the way to school? I haven't gone all week."

"Well, ye'll be goin' tomorrow, and don't think I'll be writin' any excuse for yer teacher. Ye know what Ma said about stayin' in school."

Maureen jutted out her chin. "Ma is a whole ocean away from here."

"Well, I'm standin' two feet in front of ye, and I can give ye a lickin' as good as Ma ever did."

"I'd like to see ye try." Maureen just stood there with her hands on her hips and a smug look on her face. If I let her get away with disobeyin' me, there was no tellin' what trouble she'd get into next. I smacked her good on the side of her face, knockin' her down on the feather bed.

For a few seconds she looked like a frightened little girl. I was just about to comfort her when the little vixen jumped to her feet and came at me, duckin' her head and pushin' me backward into the wall.

Then we were rollin' around the floor, each punchin' at

the other, but missin' our targets. It was a good thing we had no furniture in our room or we would have turned it into kindling.

Just when I was about exhausted, Maureen gasped, "I give up," savin' me the humiliation of bein' beat up by my little sister. I had yanked the ribbon partway out of her hair, and she lay there with half of her face covered, like a doll whose wig had come unglued.

We both lay on our backs, breathin' hard for a few minutes.

"We're a sorry pair of fighters," Maureen said.

I sat up and rubbed my bruised shoulder. "A disgrace to our fightin' Irish ancestors."

Maureen rolled over and pulled herself up on her elbows. "Rose, just listen to me for a minute. If we each had a job, we might be able to get our own place. We wouldn't have to answer to anybody."

"Even with both of us workin', we couldn't afford a whole apartment. We're better off here."

"But Mr. Garoff doesn't like us. He wants us to leave."

"That's just his way," I said. "He sounds grumpy, but I don't think he dislikes us."

"But he called us a bad name. *Shiksas.*"

"That just means girls who aren't Jewish," I said.

"Well, he didn't mean it as a compliment."

"No, I don't suppose he did."

Maureen pulled the ribbon out of her hair and retied it. "We could at least save some money and send it to Da so the rest of the family could come over sooner. But Ma hated it here so much, Rose. Do ye think she'll ever come back?"

"Da will talk her into it," I said. "Da can talk anybody into anything."

Maureen jumped to her feet. "Then it's settled. We'll stay here, but we'll save all of the money I make, and we'll send it to Da to get them over here sooner."

"Ye'll do no such thing. Ye'll go back to school tomorrow."

Maureen looked me straight in the eye. "I'm not goin' to school, Rose. There's nothin' ye can do to make me, so ye might as well let me work."

Suddenly I knew why Ma had given up that mornin' on the pier and let us stay in America. Maureen needed an education, but I couldn't sit outside the school makin' sure she stayed there. The more money we saved, the sooner the family could be together again and Maureen would be Ma's problem—and Da's. I had wanted to leave Ireland to avoid bein' a mother at a young age. A lot of good that had done. Now, instead of carin' for a sweet little baby, I was tryin' to be mother to a headstrong, big-mouthed girl. "All right," I said. "You win."

Just then the doorknob turned and Gussie came in. Maureen ran over and hugged her. "Guess what, Gussie? Rose says I can work at the Triangle from now on."

Gussie looked at me over Maureen's shoulder. "Oh, really? Well, we certainly know who's boss now, don't we?"

27

Saturday came at last. It had the feel of a special day right from the start. I decided to wear my ashes of roses dress, since we were goin' out after work.

"Isn't that a bit fancy for work?" Gussie asked.

"I want to look nice for when we go out."

Gussie shrugged. "I just hope you don't ruin it."

The minute we stepped out the door, I noticed the air felt different.

Gussie took a deep breath. "Spring at last. This is my favorite time of year. Everything seems to come to life again."

"Can we eat lunch out in the park today?" Maureen asked.

"Eat wherever ye please, as long as ye get back in on time," I said. "If ye're goin' to be a workin' girl instead of a schoolgirl, ye have to follow the rules."

"I know." Maureen skipped on ahead of us. She looked too young to be spendin' all day in a factory. I hoped I hadn't made a mistake in givin' in to her.

"When the weather gets hot this summer, we'll go to Coney Island," Gussie said.

I'd heard about the great amusement park with its roller coasters and scary rides. "Really, Gussie? Is it hard to get there?"

Gussie grinned. She was so pretty when she smiled. "It's easy. We'll take the train. Why are you looking at me like that?"

"Well, a roller coaster doesn't seem like yer cup of tea. It might be too much fun. Ye could pass out from happiness."

Gussie poked me in the arm. "Don't be silly. I like fun just as much as the next girl. I just don't indulge in it every day."

I pondered that all the way to work, tryin' to picture Gussie jumpin' waves at Coney Island.

When we reached the Asch Building, Maureen started teasin' me about not usin' the freight elevator. "Don't be silly, Rose. Try it."

"I tried it once and that was enough."

"Well, I'm not goin' to climb stairs when I can ride. They have me workin' on the eighth floor today. Where shall we meet to go to the nickelodeon? Should I wait outside the front entrance?"

"No, I don't want to be lookin' all over for ye. Come up to the ninth-floor dressing room. It usually takes Klein and Bellini a while to get ready to go." Before Maureen could say more about me bein' afraid of the elevator, I headed for the staircase and made my daily climb.

There was a lot of excited chatter when I reached the dressing room. Almost everyone had plans for the weekend. In a city like New York, there was never a lack of things to do, even if ye didn't have a lot of money. This day held two wonderful things for me—my first pay envelope and the nickelodeon. But I would have to wait until work was over for each of them.

"Nolan, come see this," Klein called. She pulled somethin' bright pink out of a bag. "It's my new suit for spring. What do you think?" She held the jacket up to herself.

"It's beautiful," I said, wonderin' if I would ever have anything so elegant.

"I have something new, too," Bellini said. She put on a straw hat with delicate pastel silk flowers tucked up under the brim so they framed her face and made her dark eyes sparkle.

"Ye could be a movie star lookin' like that," I said. "The two of ye are so fancy, ye won't want to go to the pictures with the likes of me."

Klein opened my coat. "Well, isn't this elegant?"

"My mother made it for me."

I felt proud of Ma as Bellini examined my cuff. It took a skilled seamstress to make stitches that small and even by hand.

The workday seemed to drag on endlessly. I didn't see Maureen at lunch. I figured she had gone outside to eat.

Around four o'clock, I began sneakin' looks at Mary Leventhal and Anna Gullo, to see when they would come around with the pay envelopes. Then, when I'd been concentratin' on my work, I hadn't noticed Mary makin' her way down our aisle. "Here's your pay, Rose."

"Oh, thank ye, Miss Leventhal," I said, takin' the precious envelope. I opened it and there it was, plain as day. Twelve dollars for two weeks' work! I looked up to see Klein and Bellini smilin' at me.

At four-thirty, I saw Anna Gullo headin' for the freight elevators, where the quittin' bell was. Within seconds it rang, the machines stopped, and the room filled with the sound of conversation and chairs scrapin' the floor. Freedom at last.

Klein leaned across the table. "I'm going to change my outfit for the show. Meet us in the dressing room." She and Bellini started down their aisle behind the other girls.

Gussie and I hitched our chairs forward to let several girls get by. Everyone was in a hurry on Saturdays. I opened my pay envelope again, hardly believin' I had earned so much.

"I hope you won't spend all of that right away," Gussie said.

"I suppose ye want me to use it on somethin' sensible, like union dues," I said.

"I haven't asked you to join the union."

"Not yet."

Gussie smiled. "No, not yet."

I could hear someone in the dressing room start to sing "Every Little Movement Has a Meaning All Its Own." It didn't sound like Bellini, but then I heard her join in, along with a few others. I tucked my pay in my purse. Since Gussie was still fussin' with her machine, I squeezed behind her. "I'm leavin'. I'll see ye later." I had only moved past two or three more machines when I found my way blocked by at least a dozen girls ahead of me in the narrow aisle. I should have started out right at the quittin' bell.

The tables ran all the way to the wall on one end, so everybody had to exit by the freight elevators. It had to do with the way the machines got their power, but it seemed to me they could have worked out a better arrangement. The other thing that slowed us down was that we all had to go through the one unlocked door with the guard to have our purses checked. What would we steal anyway? All any of us had was one part of a shirtwaist. What good was that?

I could hear Bellini's voice soarin' above the rest now. I thought how lucky I was to have her for a friend. I slipped my hand into my purse to make sure the pay envelope was tucked safely away. I fastened the latch, even though I would only have to open it again at the exit.

The whole line was blocked, waitin' for someone up ahead to move. Suddenly a girl screamed over by the windows. I looked to see what was wrong and saw flames outside the glass. At first it seemed like a picture show, only in color. Then I realized what was happenin'. The building was on fire!

The girls behind started pushin', but there was nowhere for me to go. When Anna Gullo shouted for everyone to be calm, the shovin' got even worse. I couldn't see Gussie. Too many girls had gone ahead of her.

The girl behind me tripped on a work basket and fell to the floor. When I tried to help her up, two girls climbed right over her and knocked me down, too. I crawled under the table and crouched there, seein' nothin' but shoes and skirts pushin' their way past me. There were loud pops and then the sound of shatterin' glass. My heart was poundin', and I couldn't make my mind work. I knew I shouldn't just hide under the table, but part of me thought it was safer than bein' carried along with the crowd. Then I saw the face of the girl who had been pushed down and trampled. Her eyes were open and bulged out of their sockets, but those eyes were past seein' anything. I screamed and buried my face in my hands.

Suddenly someone grabbed my arm and yanked me out from under the table. It was Gussie. Flames were comin' into the room now. Smoke billowed up to the ceiling. "We're goin' to die!" I screamed.

Gussie climbed on the table, pullin' me up after her. Other girls were doin' the same thing, not waitin' for the lines that were jammed in the aisles.

Gussie pointed to a door. "We'll get out that way."

I couldn't move. "Don't leave me."

Gussie smacked me hard on the cheek. "Move, or you'll burn to death." That brought me to my senses.

I followed as she jumped to the next table. Then I felt a tug on my purse. The strap had caught on one of the machines. I dropped to my knees to untangle it.

"Leave it!" Gussie yelled.

"But my pay!"

She grabbed me by the arm and yanked me off that table and onto the next. Fire was bubblin' along the machines now. A piece of lawn in the trough caught fire. The flames took one piece after another, streakin' down the whole table in seconds. The fire was movin' so fast. Why wasn't anybody tryin' to stop it?

An old woman was teetering on the edge of a table, afraid to jump off.

Gussie stopped. "Keep going, Rose. I have to help her."

"There's no time."

"Go on!" Gussie gathered up her skirt and jumped off the table, pushin' through the debris, kickin' aside a burnin' wicker basket.

Now I was alone, and the panic grabbed me again. I didn't know which way to turn. Girls were runnin' in all directions. Where were the exits? I couldn't think.

There was a strong smell like when Ma used to singe the pinfeathers off a chicken. But it wasn't feathers. I felt the heat at the top of my head. My hair was on fire! I screamed and tried to beat out the flames with my hands.

A machinist grabbed a pail of water and dumped it over my head. The shock of it took my breath away. He grabbed my arm and pulled me toward a door. But when we got there, he couldn't open it. "It's locked," he said, smashin' his fist against it. "They have us locked in!"

The worktables were all burnin' now, and the smoke had

filled the room almost down to the level of our heads. There were a few girls still sittin' at their machines, held fast by their fear, with flames all around them. I was torn between savin' them and findin' a way out, which left me stumblin' helplessly in circles. The smoke burned my throat, and my eyes were stingin' so bad I could hardly see. The fire roared like a train, and girls were screamin' all over the room.

Suddenly I heard someone shoutin' my name. Bellini and Klein were in a crowd of girls over by the windows. I ran to them, and we clung to each other. "The windows are the only way out now," Klein said, chokin' on the smoke. "Come on." She started to climb up on the sill.

I grabbed her arm. "Have ye lost your mind? That's a nine-story drop."

Klein clutched the edge of the window and stood up. "It's all right. I can hear fire wagons. They'll save us."

Bellini and I leaned on the windowsill. Klein was right. Fire whistles and bells were comin' from all directions. But some of the girls weren't waitin' for them. Two men had taken the blankets from their horses and got others from the crowd to stretch them out. "Jump!" they called. "We'll catch you."

"We'll wait for the firemen," Klein said. "They'll take us down the ladders."

A girl a few windows away jumped for a horse blanket. When she landed, the impact tore the blanket from the men's hands, and she landed hard on the pavement. Other men were runnin' out with tarps and blankets, but they couldn't save the fallin' bodies.

The first fire truck stopped right under us and started to raise its ladder. Bellini was sobbin', but Klein stayed calm. "Hang on a few more minutes."

I was thinkin' they'd better hurry, because the heat was almost unbearable. My dress and petticoat had been soaked by the bucket of water, but now I felt dry in the back clear through to my legs. The ladder rose slowly, then stopped several floors below us. "They can't reach us," I cried.

A girl jumped for the ladder, missed, and streaked like a flamin' comet to the street.

Bellini sobbed uncontrollably. Klein gripped her hand. "They have huge safety nets. They'll catch us."

Bellini pulled away from the window. "I can't. It's too far."

"We'll all hold hands," Klein said. "We'll jump together."

"If we're jumpin', let's go," I shouted. I gave Bellini a boost up to the windowsill and pulled myself up next to her. When I looked down, I almost lost my balance. Then the smoke billowed out from the floor below so I couldn't see the ground for a moment. I tried to get a gulp of fresh air, but I was too terrified to take a deep breath. As we gripped each other for dear life, a girl jumped. The sudden movement made me feel like I was fallin', and I held on tighter to Bellini. As the girl dropped, the firemen moved their safety net under her, shoutin' encouragement.

"See?" Klein shouted. "It's like stepping off a curb." The girl landed in the middle of the net, then bounced high and crumpled into a lifeless heap on the pavement.

"It doesn't work!" I screamed. "We're too high up for the nets."

Girls were pressin' in behind us now. "Jump or get out of the way!" one of them screamed.

But before we could jump, three girls in the next window clasped hands and stepped off the sill. The smolderin' hair of one of the girls broke into flames on the way down. A group of firemen rushed a safety net under them. I held my breath. How would it feel to fall that far?

Then the girls broke right through the net. And through the sidewalk below—the sidewalk with the little glass windows.

Klein's hand went to her throat. "My God! They can't save us!"

"I'm not jumpin'!" I shouted.

Klein reached in front of Bellini for my hand. "Don't burn, Nolan." She was coughin' so hard she could barely speak. "We'll die together."

"No!" Bellini sobbed.

I felt them start to go over the edge. I couldn't tell if they meant to jump, or if Klein had lost her balance reachin' for me.

"Don't!" I screamed, pullin' away.

Bellini's hand clawed at my sleeve, but I clung to the window frame with both hands.

And I watched my best friends drop all the way to the pavement.

28

    As I tried to get back into the room, I was almost pushed backward out of the window by the girls tryin' to jump. There was a huge crowd fightin' to get to the windows now, and I saw why. The flames had cut the room in half. On the other side of the fire, I could see a crowd of people over by the passenger elevators. A girl in front of me tried to run through the flames. Within seconds her hair and clothes were on fire. She stood twistin' in the orange flame like a dancer. Then she crumpled to the floor.

I was so terrified watchin' someone die, I had bitten into my knuckle until I tasted blood. But that was the only way to escape. I had to run into the fire or die right where I was. I ran to a pole holdin' fire buckets and found one that was still full. I dumped it over myself, pulled the back of my soggy skirt up over my head and ran straight into the fire. It was like bein' in a bad dream. I couldn't see anything but flames. Was I goin' in the right direction? I seemed to be movin' so slowly. There was no air. Could I hold my breath long enough to get through the fire? Suddenly I slammed into somethin'. It was the crowd of girls by the elevator. I had made it!

There were screams up front as one of the elevators started down. Had I run through fire only to burn now? I was almost ready to give up when the other elevator came back up. I pushed hard to get to the door, but just as I reached it, the elevator started down. The girl next to me lost her balance and fell, arms like windmills in the air. She landed headfirst on the top of the elevator.

I felt like I was back on the windowsill. I couldn't make myself jump, but the crowd was pushin' me. I stretched out my arms, clingin' to both sides of the open door. I tried to brace myself. There was too much pressure. I was bein' shoved into the open shaft. Flames shot out from the floor below. This was the elevator's last trip. It was either jump for my life or be pushed to my death. I leaned back against the crowd as I wound my wet skirt several times around each hand like bandages.

Then I crouched and jumped for the elevator cable the way I used to dive for the swingin' rope at Boys Sandy. I gripped hard with my hands and wrapped my legs around the cable, slidin' down until I could drop to the top of the elevator. Even that short slide had almost worn through the fabric I'd wrapped around my hands. Then somethin' hit my shoulder, knockin' me flat on my back. It was another girl, landin' unconscious next to me. As we descended, I saw a fireman through the grill in the stairwell. "Help me!" I cried.

"You'll be all right," he called back. But he couldn't see what I saw. The top of the shaft was filled with flame. Girls were comin' down like torches. I rolled to the front wall of the elevator so I wouldn't be hit by the fallin' bodies.

I closed my eyes, listenin' to them land, one after another. Thud. Thud. Thud. The whole car shuddered with each one. I wondered how many more could land on us before the cable broke from the weight. But I knew if I had made it this far I could survive.

That's when I remembered somethin' terrible.

I remembered Maureen.

29

The weight of all the people made the elevator sink to the bottom of the shaft. Once, when we passed by a door that had been pried open, I had to hold on to the lifeless girl next to me to keep from rollin' out. I felt my dress rip as the skirt got caught in the opening. Finally, we stopped, and I could see several firemen in the open lobby elevator door above me. I scrambled to my feet. "Please, help me!"

I reached up my hands and they lifted me out. I started for the stairwell, and one fireman caught me around the waist. "You can't go up there."

"I have to find my little sister."

Another fireman came over. Tears had made white streaks in his sooty face. "You can't do anything. They're all past saving up there."

"No!" I tried to wrestle free, but they each grabbed an

arm and led me to the door, where we were stopped by another fireman.

He was lookin' up. "Wait here for a moment. They're still coming down." I thought he meant the elevators, but then I saw a burnin' bundle hit the sidewalk, and from the sound of it, I knew it wasn't just fabric. A crowd of Triangle girls were huddled in the doorway, sobbin'. I waited until nobody was watchin' me, and then I ran out and across the street.

The whole top three floors were ablaze, and the smoke made the sky as dark as night. A fireman unharnessed a team of wild-eyed horses from the fire wagon and handed the reins to a policeman. "Get them around the corner. The smell of blood has them spooked." I looked down to see that the stream of water runnin' close to the curb was stained red. And then I saw the bodies. They were all over the street and sidewalk, some by themselves, some in piles where they had landed on top of one another. Was one of them Maureen?

I tried to get to the nearest group to look for her, but a policeman stopped me. "You don't want to see that," he said.

"I have to find my sister. She needs me."

"If she's over there, she doesn't need anybody." When I groaned at his remark, he took me gently in his arms and spoke softly in my ear. "Why don't you go home so your parents don't worry about you? Your sister is probably with them right now."

I sobbed into his shoulder. "No. I left her. I left her in the fire."

Another pair of fire horses reared up in terror right behind us, and the policeman let go of me to catch their reins so they wouldn't trample the crowd. I stumbled on down the block, lookin' at faces, hopin' to see Maureen. She was young and strong. And hadn't she said, back when we were out on Uncle Patrick's fire escape, that she would never jump, not even from the lowest platform of a fire escape?

I kept runnin' the facts through my mind. The fire had started right at quittin' time. Maureen wouldn't have had time to come up to the ninth floor. And there were lots of men on the eighth—the cutters. Surely one of them would have taken a young girl under his wing and led her down the stairs to safety.

I had to push my way through crowds of people who were streamin' into Washington Square. There couldn't be this many people with relatives workin' at the Triangle. Some of these people were comin' just to look, to stare at the broken bodies as if they were goin' to the nickelodeon for entertainment. "Go home," I screamed, barely able to see through my tears. "It's none of yer business."

As I ran block after block, I kept sayin' over and over, "Please, God, let Maureen be all right; please, God . . ." as if repeatin' the words would make it happen.

I tripped on a curb, sprawlin' in the middle of the street. Several men ran out to help me, but I scrambled to my feet and pushed away their hands. I finally reached our building and ran up the stairs. "Maureen!" I screamed. When I opened the door, the apartment was dark. I ran into our room, callin' out again. She wasn't there. I threw myself on the feather bed and tried to pull the edges up over me. Ma had trusted me to take care of Maureen. And now what had I done?

Why hadn't I thought of Maureen in the fire? Was she in one of those crowds I had pushed through? Had I shoved my own sister aside to save myself? Had I left her there to die? "Oh, Ma!" I cried. "I'm so sorry. I meant to take good care of her."

Pictures of the fire kept goin' through my mind. I pressed my fists against my eyes to make them go away, but I could still see the faces of Klein and Bellini goin' over the window ledge. I hadn't tried to save them, either. I had just hung on to the window to save myself. I was a terrible person. I wrapped myself tighter in the feather bed and wailed.

But stayin' here wasn't helpin' Maureen. As much as I dreaded it, I had to go back there. I wrapped myself in the shawl that Gussie had lent me the day she took me back to Mr. Moscovitz's shop. Gussie! I hadn't given her a thought, either. And Mr. Garoff. Was he out lookin' for her? Surely everybody had heard about the fire by now. The smoke must have been seen for miles.

When I got outside, people were streamin' through the streets. These weren't thrill seekers. I caught snatches of conversation. "I told her not to work there." "I knew something terrible would happen." "My poor Rachel."

As I approached the fire scene, I slowed down, and

people jostled me, rushin' past. I didn't know if I could face that awful sight again, but I had to find Maureen. And Gussie. Where was Gussie?

I found a line of policemen holdin' back the crowd that was pressin' in from Washington Square. I tried to work my way through to the front, searchin' faces as I went. I didn't see anyone I knew from work.

Then someone called out the name "Bessie" in an agonized cry. The crowd surged forward to the bodies. There were screams and moans and prayers, and above it all, the shouts of policemen tellin' them to go back. I was carried with them along Washington Place and around the corner to Greene Street, where I managed to stumble out of the crowd.

This was where I would be lyin' now if I had jumped with Klein and Bellini. I made myself look at the pile of bodies and thought I saw the bright pink of Klein's new suit. When I got closer, I found it was another girl, whose white blouse had been stained with blood.

A policeman took me roughly by the arm and pulled me back.

"Please," I said, "I've lost my sister."

"I'm sorry, miss. We'll be taking all the . . . We'll be settin' up a morgue . . . a place where you can . . . Look, you shouldn't be doin' this alone. Go find your parents. Let them help you."

My parents! How I wished I could run into Da's arms and feel safe. He would find Maureen and he would take us

217

home to an apartment of our own, where we could be a family again.

As I turned away, I stepped on something soft. It was a bonnet, soaked and crushed—a spring straw bonnet with pastel silk flowers tucked up under the brim. I dropped to my knees, hugged the bonnet to my chest, and sobbed.

30

❧ *I couldn't leave* the scene of the fire. I didn't want to go back to that empty apartment. I watched as the firemen spread a dark-red canvas over the Greene Street sidewalk across the street from the Asch Building. Then they worked in pairs, carefully liftin' the bodies and placin' them on the canvas. I was waitin' to see a body that was smaller than the others. I was waitin' for them to find Maureen.

I didn't cry anymore. I was numb, as if what was goin' on had nothin' to do with me. I watched as wagons brought in wooden caskets, dozens of them. I watched as they carefully put a body in each one, then loaded the pine boxes into ambulances and patrol wagons. The crowd parted as the clangin' death wagons took them away.

Then darkness fell, and two fire trucks with searchlights were brought in. I saw firemen on the roof lower a hook to the ninth floor of the Greene Street side, where several firemen pulled it into a window. When they let it swing out again, it held a long, slender wrapped bundle. There was a moan from the crowd as they realized what it was.

Firemen on the Washington Place side were doin' the same thing. Spotlights followed the bodies as they twisted and turned at the end of the cable. At each floor, a fireman leaned out of the window to keep the body from hittin' the building. Such care was bein' taken now that it was too late. Why hadn't anyone cared enough to make sure this couldn't happen in the first place?

The sad bundles were lowered down each side of the building, like an eerie trapeze performance. These were the girls I had worked with every day, had shared laughs with in the dressing room.

There was a policeman pickin' up personal belongings—shoes, combs, purses. I clutched the hat, knowin' I should give it up but wantin' to keep it. I could give it to Bellini's family, if I ever met them.

Around eight o'clock, the firemen carried a man out of the Greene Street entrance. They put him in an ambulance, which took off at a furious speed, bell clangin'. I heard someone say he had been alive, under one of the elevators in the basement. He had almost drowned as the water from the fire hoses rose.

Workers from the Edison Company arrived and strung rows of arc lights along both streets, makin' a little patch of daylight in the night. Then they went inside and put lights on every floor. Now we could see gigantic shadows runnin' across the ceiling as the firemen carried on their search. From somewhere inside, a burglar alarm had been triggered. Nobody bothered to turn it off, so it continued to ring while body after body was lowered.

I heard two women talkin' about goin' to the Mercer Street Police Station, where they were givin' out information about the dead and injured, so I followed them. Many others made the three-block walk to the station. It was somethin' to do, better than standin' helplessly. But when we got there, a policeman at the door told us that the bodies were bein' taken to a morgue on a pier at Twenty-sixth Street.

"I'm tryin' to find my little sister," I said. "She's only twelve."

"We don't have her here," the policeman said, "but we have some of the personal articles from the girls. You can look and see if there is anything of hers."

I went inside to a table filled with shoes, purses, hats, and combs. Two policemen were makin' sure nobody stole anything. I couldn't find any signs of Maureen. Then I saw a patch of taffeta about the size of a handkerchief. Even though it was wet I recognized the color. It was ashes of roses and matched the piece of my skirt that had been torn away in the elevator shaft. I had to grip the table. The sight of somethin' of mine among the relics of the dead made the room swirl.

"Are you all right?" asked the policeman across from me. "Did you find something to identify?"

I pointed to the fabric, then lifted the hem of my skirt to show him the ripped place. "This is mine. I'm alive."

He handed me the scrap. "Thank God. I hope we find more like you."

As I turned and headed for the door, two girls I recognized came into the police station. It was Bertha and Esther. I had met them in the park my first day at the Triangle. I ran over to them. "Ye work on the eighth floor, don't ye? Did ye see my little sister? She just started there today." So few girls worked on the eighth, I hoped they might have noticed her.

"The pretty little one with the pale-blue eyes?" Bertha asked, her eyes red from cryin'.

"Yes, that's her."

"I think she left before the fire started. She was excited about something she was supposed to do tonight."

"Then ye think she got out all right?"

"If she left the building right away she would have been safe," Esther said. "The fire started right in front of us, in a bin under one of the cutters' tables. Then it blazed up and caught all the patterns that were hanging on a wire over the table. I was going to throw a pail of water on it, but Mr. Bernstein told all us girls to get out."

"Have you seen Gussie?" Bertha asked.

"I haven't seen her since the fire," I said.

Esther shook her head. "She never should have left the eighth floor. I think all of our girls escaped. The men stayed to fight the fire, but we girls got out."

I thanked them and turned away, tears blurrin' my eyes. I knew that Maureen didn't leave the building right away. She ran up the stairs to the ninth-floor dressing room, because that's what I told her to do. If she had waited for us outside, the way she wanted to, she would have been safe. But I had sent her right into the fire. And Gussie bein' on the ninth floor was my fault, too. If I hadn't made her late that mornin' three weeks ago, she would have escaped. I might have killed them both.

I turned and ran back to the fire scene. And now I called Maureen's name, screamin' like a madwoman. Then I heard a woman's voice call, "Rose!" Was it Gussie? Did she have Maureen?

"I'm here!" I shouted. We kept callin' back and forth while I pushed my way through the crowd. My heart was poundin' with joy as the voice got closer and closer. I followed it, squeezin' around the last person only to come face-to-face with a woman I'd never seen before. We stared at each other in bitter disappointment, then both burst into tears.

I went past the building without lookin' at it this time. The shrill ring of the burglar alarm seemed to drill right into my skull. Why didn't someone turn it off? I moved through the crowd toward the park, callin' out Maureen's name and Gussie's, but not expectin' an answer.

Finally, I climbed up on a park bench so I could see over the crowd. Then I spotted them—a dazed old man bein' led by a young girl. I leapt off the bench, ran to them, and hugged my little sister at last.

"Rose!" Maureen sobbed. "Oh, Rose, I thought ye were dead."

I picked her up. "Thank heaven ye're safe." I carried her back to the bench and held her on my lap, rockin' her like a baby as she sobbed into my shoulder.

Mr. Garoff followed and sat next to me. "My Gussela. She was with you, no?"

"No, Mr. Garoff. I haven't seen her since . . ." In my mind I saw Gussie goin' back for the old Italian woman, kickin' aside that burnin' basket.

"She is all right? She came out of the building with you?" His eyes looked so pained, I couldn't hurt him.

I pushed aside my doubts. "I'm sure she's fine, Mr. Garoff. Gussie can take care of herself."

"Too much she takes care of herself. She needs someone to take care of her."

I thought that Gussie's real problem was that she tried to take care of everybody but herself, but I only said, "Thank you for finding Maureen, Mr. Garoff."

His eyes searched the crowd. "We found each other . . . wandering, looking."

I hugged Maureen. "How did ye get out? I was so afraid that ye came up to the ninth floor."

"I did, but the fire had started and a man yelled to me that I should go on up to the roof."

"The roof! How did ye get down from there?"

"Some students from the university put a ladder across from their building. They helped us all get across. Before

224

they got there, one girl jumped." She started cryin' again. "I couldn't do it, Rose. I couldn't jump."

I held her close, her cheek pressed against mine so I could feel her hot tears. "I know, Maureen. I couldn't jump, either. Thank heaven we didn't." Who would have thought that university students cared enough to save my sister? Things were not always as they seemed in America.

Mr. Garoff stood up. "I think Gussela is not all right. In my heart I know that . . ." His face crumpled and he let out a choked sob. "They say there is a place where we can look. A place where they take the . . . girls."

I put my hand on his arm. "Maybe if we go back to the apartment, Mr. Garoff, Gussie will be waiting for us."

The look in his eyes broke my heart. "She waits, but not at home. A father knows these things. I go now to find my Gussela."

31

🌹 "*Where are we goin'?*" Maureen whispered. We were followin' a few steps behind Mr. Garoff, movin' along with the huge crowd that was headed for the pier on East Twenty-sixth Street.

"We're goin' to the morgue. That's where they've taken the bodies."

"Is Gussie dead?"

"I don't know. She went back into the fire to help someone instead of savin' herself. But she's so strong, I think she could have gotten out alive."

Maureen stopped and pulled on my arm. "Do we have to go and look at the dead bodies?"

"I can't leave Mr. Garoff alone, Maureen. Go back to the apartment and wait for us, if ye want."

"I'm afraid to be by myself," Maureen said. "I'll come."

"All right. Ye don't have to go inside with us."

I took her hand, and we ran to catch up with Mr. Garoff. He didn't look up as we stepped up beside him. I had never seen so many people in the streets before. The crowd was like a restless animal, movin' just because it couldn't stay still.

As we walked up First Avenue, I realized we must be fairly close to Uncle Patrick's. Part of me wanted to break away from the crowd and go to his apartment, where we could be helped and comforted. But Mr. Garoff needed help and comfort right now, especially if we found Gussie in the morgue. I decided to stay with him.

The police had set up a barricade at First Avenue and Twenty-sixth Street, and the crowd was growin' behind it. Every now and then a wagon would come through with more bodies. In spite of the police wieldin' clubs and shoutin' at them, people barely parted enough to let them pass, closin' in right after they went by. Mothers screamed and tore at the blankets coverin' the bodies. Each time, the wailin' and cryin' would hit a high pitch, then die out just in time to be set off by the next wagon. It was more terrible than the worst nightmare I had ever had. As we walked along, I kept reachin' out to touch Maureen to remind myself that we were both alive.

Finally, the police announced they would be lettin' people into the morgue at midnight. They formed the crowd into two lines, four or five abreast. Then a policeman came down between the lines callin' out, "Kaplan? Is anyone looking for a girl whose pay envelope says Kaplan?"

227

A woman down the line from us screamed and was led into the morgue supported by her family.

"Anyone looking for a girl whose ring bears the initials G. G.?" asked another policeman.

I caught my breath. Those were Gussie's initials. Gussela Garoff. I was almost afraid to ask. "Did Gussie have a ring like that, Mr. Garoff?"

He kept his head bowed. "No, no rings. No jewelry."

Finally, the line started to move, but it was still a long time before we reached the door. They were lettin' people enter the building in groups of twenty. Several policemen went in with each group. As long as we had waited, our turn came before I had steeled myself for the ordeal we had ahead of us. I took a deep breath. "Wait here, Maureen. I'll come find ye as soon as we're finished."

She hesitated, but then grabbed my hand. "No, I'll come with ye."

"Are ye sure?"

She nodded.

"All right, then. Stay close." I gripped her hand tight, mostly because I was terrified.

We went into a large, dark room with sputterin' arc lights overhead that seemed to throw more shadows than illumination. The bodies were arranged in two long rows, in pine coffins, with their heads propped up awkwardly on boards so you could see their faces. I thought about how uncomfortable that looked, then realized it didn't matter. I squeezed Maureen's hand to keep my mind from seein' her laid out like this.

It wasn't long before I recognized the faces of two girls who sat in the next row over from me at work. I knew the pretty one had just gotten engaged last week. She had come down our row showin' off her ring, and I had admired it. And now there it was, glitterin' on her finger as she lay in her coffin.

As we moved down the row, the girls in the pine boxes began to seem more like life-sized dolls than real people to me. Maybe tellin' myself that was the only way I could bear lookin' at them. Mr. Garoff had gone on ahead of us.

Then my heart almost stopped at the sight of two more familiar faces. I let out a cry, and a policeman came to my side. "You found the girl you were looking for?" His lantern showed their faces in full light.

Maureen buried her face in my coat. "Klein and Bellini! Oh, Rose, I can't look."

Bellini's head was turned slightly to the side, and her face wore an expression of sheer terror. Poor Bellini. She had been so afraid of jumpin'. Why hadn't I grabbed for her?

"Miss? Do you know this girl? Are you related?" The policeman moved the lantern to Klein's face. Her eyes were starin' right at me, and her mouth was open as if she was about to say somethin'. Her body and clothes weren't burned, but her hand was raised toward her face and twisted at a strange angle.

"Miss? If you know her name . . . We need to get their names to notify the families."

I choked down a sob. "Her name is Rose Klein. And the girl next to her is Rose Bellini."

He wrote the names in his notebook. "Both named Rose," he said, shakin' his head. "Can you give me their addresses?"

I burst into tears. "They were my best friends, but I don't know where they lived."

My knees started to buckle, and I almost pulled Maureen down with me, but the policeman caught us both. "Did you come here with someone, miss?"

"The girls are with me." I looked up to see Mr. Garoff comin' back for us. He took Maureen's hand and put his arm around my waist to hold me up. "Do you need to go outside?"

"No," I gasped. "This is just so awful."

"It is terrible to lose friends," he said, his voice hoarse, "especially ones so young." He held me quietly for a few minutes, until I felt steady enough to keep goin'.

It didn't take long to figure out that the bodies in the best condition had been placed closest to the door. As we moved farther back into the building, they were more badly burned and harder to recognize. Maureen wouldn't look at the faces. She clung to me and kept her head down, seein' only the feet of the girls we passed. Mr. Garoff stopped to look in each coffin, shakin' his head and mutterin' what sounded like prayers.

We had made our way almost to the end of the building. "I don't think she's here," I whispered to Mr. Garoff. "Maybe we should check the hospitals."

"You go, if you want. I keep looking." His voice was barely a whisper now.

I wanted to get out of there. I couldn't breathe. There were screams and moans all over the building as people found their loved ones.

Then Maureen cried out in horror. "Oh, no! Here she is! This is Gussie."

She was lookin' at the feet of a girl who was so badly burned, her face looked like lumps of coal. I had to turn away. "There's no way to tell who that is."

I tried to push Maureen ahead, but she stood her ground, sobbin'. "I know it's Gussie. Look at her shoe. It has that steel plate on the heel."

"*Gottenyu!*" Mr. Garoff dropped to his knees and gripped the foot of the coffin. "My Gussela! My *shaineh* Gussela!" he wailed.

Two men came runnin' over to us when they heard his cries. They called Mr. Garoff by name and crouched down next to him, speakin' in Yiddish.

It wasn't until that moment that I realized how much I had been countin' on Gussie to comfort me—to make everything all right again. She would know what to say. She could tell us what we were supposed to do. Maureen and I clung to each other. Nothin' made sense. Gussie couldn't be dead. She was the strong one.

Now that Mr. Garoff didn't need our help anymore, I felt a panic take over me. I grabbed Maureen's hand and ran headlong out of the building, all the way to the end of the pier.

"Rose, what are ye doin'?" Maureen cried, tryin' to hold me back.

I dropped to my knees and vomited into the water. When I finished, Maureen and I held each other and cried.

"What are we goin' to do, Rose?"

"I'm not sure." I didn't even know what I'd be doin' tomorrow, much less weeks and months from now. Still, I didn't want to frighten Maureen. She was only a child, and it was my fault that we were in this mess.

Maureen wiped her eyes. "Well, I've been doin' a lot of thinkin'. Ye know Ma and Da are never comin' back here, don't ye?"

The matter-of-fact way she said it made me realize she was right. I probably had known it since Ma left us on the pier. So much for protectin' Maureen from the hard truth. "I know," I said. "Ma hates it here. She'll talk Da into stayin' in Limerick."

"So what do ye think we should do," Maureen asked, "stay here or go back? I've been thinkin' about that, too, and Uncle Patrick could help us out either way."

When had Maureen changed from a little ninny into this girl who made me feel like the younger sister? "Everything happened too fast," I said. "I need time to figure it out. Let's go back to our room."

As we walked through the streets, still crowded as if it were the middle of the day, I was lost in thought. We had gone to work this mornin' without a care in the world. How could everything have changed in just a few hours?

"D'ye know what I think?" Maureen asked, when we were almost home.

"What?"

"We should stay here in America. I think we'll be all right from now on. Because, as long as we live, we'll never have another day as terrible as the twenty-fifth of March 1911."

32

🌹 *By the time we got back* to the apartment, a faint light was showin' in the sky over the East River. And as we walked down the hall, we heard voices comin' from behind the door.

"Do ye think we should go in?" Maureen asked.

"Of course. We live here, don't we?" But I felt uneasy as I turned the knob. We weren't family, just people who paid to use some space. I thought maybe we shouldn't intrude, but I was exhausted and cold and wanted the comfort of Ma's feather bed.

Mr. Garoff was sittin' at the table with his face in his hands. The two men from the morgue plus an older woman were with him.

The woman got up as we came into the room. "Oh, you poor dears. What a horrible thing you've gone through." She steered me into her seat, then turned and took Maureen's face in her hands. "Oh, and this one. So young. Where is your mama?"

"I am," I said. "I mean, I'm takin' care of her. We're sisters."

The woman poked one of the men, who got up and gave Maureen his chair. "Just a child herself," she clucked. "How could we let our young girls work for such monsters?" She went to the stove and poured tea for us. "Here, a *glezel tai* to warm yourselves. Are you hungry?" Without waitin' for an answer, she cut thick slices of black bread and set them next to the tea.

Mr. Garoff looked up and took my hand in his. He tried to say somethin', but just shook his head, tears runnin' down his cheeks. I put my other hand over his. "I'm so sorry about Gussie, Mr. Garoff." He closed his eyes and nodded, but I felt him squeeze my hand. My heart broke for him.

The woman, whose name we learned was Leah, watched over us as we tried to choke down some food. The men continued their discussion in Yiddish. "They're planning for the *leveiyeh*," she whispered, "the funeral."

When we finished, Maureen went to Mr. Garoff. He looked up at her for a second, then hugged her. "You're a good girl," he whispered, pattin' her back. "A good little girl."

Leah went into our room with us and fluffed up the feather bed. "Get some sleep, now."

"I'm afraid to go to sleep," Maureen said.

I realized I was afraid of sleep, too. When I closed my eyes, would I see the fire? I felt as if all those horrible images were right there waitin' for me, lurkin' behind my eyelids. Would I ever be able to forget the things I'd seen?

Leah sat beside Maureen on the bed and put her arm around her. "It's all right, *maideleh.* Nothing can happen to you now." She started singin' a song in Yiddish, then reached out her other arm to include me. And though I thought I'd never be able to sleep again, the last thing I remembered was Leah quietly slippin' out of bed and tuckin' the covers over Maureen and me.

When I awoke the next mornin', the first thought that went through my mind was the fire. As I tried to get out of bed, I felt the bruises on my knees from landin' on the elevator and burns on my hands from beatin' at the fire in my hair. There were more burns on the backs of my legs. They must have been unprotected when I ran through the fire with the back of my wet skirt pulled up over my head. Maureen seemed to be sleepin' soundly, so I didn't disturb her.

When I went out into the kitchen, I was surprised to find Leah sittin' at the table. "Good morning, Rose. How are you feeling?"

"All right," I said. I certainly wasn't goin' to mention my small ailments. After all, I was alive.

She set out tea with bread and cheese for me. "The others have gone with Mr. Garoff to make the funeral arrangements."

Leah carried on a one-sided conversation while I ate. I learned that she and her grown daughter ran a deli in our neighborhood. They belonged to the same synagogue as Mr. Garoff, and so did the two men from the morgue.

Maureen wandered in sleepy-eyed and sat next to me, leanin' against my shoulder. I pushed her hair out of her eyes and kissed her on the forehead. "Are you all right this mornin'?"

She nodded and reached for the glass of tea Leah had put in front of her.

"You sure?" I asked. "No burns?"

"I told you," Maureen said. "I never saw the fire. I went right up to the roof."

Leah looked at me. "Rose? Did you get burned?"

"It was nothin'," I said.

"Let me see." She took my hands in hers and turned them palm-up. "Why didn't you tell me last night? You have some blisters here. Anywhere else?"

"A little on my legs. It's all right."

Leah emptied the contents of her purse on the table. "I have something for burns." From the number of things that tumbled out of her purse, I thought she must have somethin' for everything. She caught a little jar that almost rolled off the table edge and plucked a small roll of bandages from the pile.

"Are you a nurse?" Maureen asked.

"No. I just like to be prepared." The salve took away the sting as she spread it on my burns. Then she neatly wound the bandages.

"You could be a nurse if you wanted to," Maureen said, impressed.

I finished the last of my bread and cheese. "What will become of Mr. Garoff?" I asked.

"He's going back to Russia," Leah said. "There's nothing here for him now."

"Wouldn't it be better to bring his family over here?" Maureen asked.

Leah shook her head. "This is the way he wanted it. He said America's streets weren't paved in gold after all. He wants to be back with his family in the village where he was born. A worker from the Women's Trade Union League was here this morning. They're going to pay for Gussie's funeral and for his passage back home."

I thought it was sad that Mr. Garoff was leavin' America. Even with all we had gone through, I wouldn't want to go back to Ireland for good. But I did long to see Ma and Da.

When Leah was sure that Maureen and I were all right, she went home.

"Will Mr. Garoff and those men be bringin' Gussie back here?" Maureen asked.

"I don't know."

"Well, I don't want to be here if they do."

"Neither do I. Let's go for a walk." I didn't mean to be disrespectful, but I couldn't look at Gussie again. I wanted to remember her face the way it used to be.

When I combed my hair, I could feel that it was all short

pieces on the top, where it had been burned. The mirror had been covered with a black cloth, so I couldn't see what I was doin'. I knew the cloth must have somethin' to do with Gussie's death, so I didn't touch it.

"Sit down," Maureen said. "I'll help you." She pulled up the long hair and twisted it in a bun on top to cover the burned place. She stepped back to examine her handiwork. "You look older."

"I feel ancient," I said.

As we walked through the neighborhood, three funeral processions passed us. There were crowds of weepin' family and friends followin' each one. On every block, there was at least one door with flowers tacked to it. I stopped when we reached the street where Klein had lived—Spring Street. Why couldn't I remember that when the policeman asked me for her address? I didn't know which building she lived in, though. From the corner, I could see three with flowers on their doors.

Maureen looked up. "What's the matter, Rose?"

"This is the street Klein lived on."

"Do ye want to look for her family?"

A picture of Klein's laughin' face ran through my mind. "No. There's too much sadness here."

When we neared Washington Square, the streets were crowded. "What are all these people doin' here?" Maureen asked.

"I don't know." Though I hadn't been thinkin' about it,

it was obvious that I was headin' to the scene of the fire. I didn't know why. Maybe I needed to see the building to know that the fire had really happened.

"Look," Maureen shouted, pointin' to a figure in the crowd. "It's Jacob!"

Hearin' his name, Jacob turned, then ran toward us.

"Rose! Maureen! You're alive!" He hugged both of us, and though I thought I had no tears left, I sobbed with him. He finally led us over to a park bench where we could sit together. "Did you see the newspapers? A hundred and forty-six people died."

"Oh, Jacob, how did you get out?"

"I was the first one out at the quitting bell. The fire must have started just after I left." He ran his hands through his hair, lookin' distraught, then broke down again. "I ran back when I heard the fire sirens. By the time I got here, the girls were jumping." He covered his eyes for a second or two, then looked up at me. "Did you see Gussie, Rose? Was she one of the ones . . ."

"No, Jacob. Gussie didn't jump."

He took in a sharp breath, then let it out slowly. "That thought haunted me all night. If she was one of the girls I saw jumping. If I could have run out and broken her fall . . ."

"No one could catch them," I said. "Not even the firemen with safety nets. It was hopeless."

His eyes teared up again. "Did you see? Do you know how she . . . what happened to her?"

He looked so pained, I put my hand on his arm. "Gussie saved me, Jacob. Without her, I would have burned. Last I saw of her, she went back to rescue an old woman."

He shook his head. "Why did she always put others before herself?" He noticed the bandage on my hand. "You were hurt, Rose? How did you get out?"

I pulled my hand away. "It's nothin'. I took the elevator." That wasn't really a lie. I didn't want to relive the escape by talkin' about it. "Jacob, I have somethin' terrible to confess. It was my fault that Gussie died. I was responsible for her bein' moved to the ninth floor. I made her late for work that day and . . ."

"Rose, Gussie never did anything she didn't want to do. She could have asked Bernstein for her old job back. You had nothing to do with her death."

"But why didn't she go back downstairs?"

"Who knows?" Jacob looked away, and I could see he was strugglin' not to cry. "Did Gussie tell you I asked her to marry me?"

"No. I had no idea."

He looked at me, his eyes filled with tears again. "She wouldn't even let me talk to her father about it. She just kept saying, 'Not yet,' whatever that meant. Gussie had a mind of her own."

"I'm sorry, Jacob," Maureen said, takin' his hand. "I didn't know about you and Gussie."

"Nobody did." Jacob lifted his chin and tried to smile, but his face crumpled again. "I can't imagine life without her."

I stood up and took his other hand. "Maybe you'll feel better if we walk." There were no words to help Jacob's pain, but I couldn't sit still any longer. I felt so helpless. I needed to be doin' somethin', even if it was only walkin'.

The three of us started across Washington Square. A procession of Fifth Avenue stage buses were bringin' people to the park. Their open tops were filled with young couples laughin' and chattin' as they went to view the tragedy. The women were dressed to the nines, with bright feathered and flowered hats. They were doin' this as a lark—just a little entertainment for a Sunday mornin'. I could feel a rage risin' up in me.

A man at the edge of Washington Square sold candy apples from a cart, glad for the extra customers. He held one out to me, but I pushed past him without a word.

It was the next vendor who set me off. He shoved a tray of small envelopes and matchboxes in front of me. "Buy a dead girl's earrings? How about a ring from a dead girl's finger?"

I knocked the tray out of his hands. The boxes fell open when they hit the sidewalk, and their contents were scooped up by eager sightseers. It wasn't real jewelry at all, just cheap glass and paste imitations. I was sure not one of these fakes had belonged to a Triangle worker. I didn't know if that made me feel better or worse.

The man raised his hand to strike me. "Thief!"

Jacob had the man on the ground in the flash of an eye.

"You're lower than a worm," he growled. He pulled the man to his feet by his jacket collar and shoved him into the crowd. Jacob was still shakin' from anger as he came back to us.

"Why would anybody do such a thing?" I sputtered. I turned to a group of fancy couples who were starin' at us. One of the girls was laughin' behind her fan and pointin' at Jacob. My anger spilled over. I went right up to her. "Did ye know that fancy shirtwaist ye're wearin' was made at the Triangle? So ye have yer precious souvenir from the fire. Ye can go home now and tell all yer snooty friends that ye're wearin' a waist made by a dead girl's hands."

The girl put her gloved hand to her throat, and her boyfriend rushed her away from me. The rest of their group retreated toward Fifth Avenue.

"Gussie would have been impressed by that little speech," Jacob said with a sad smile.

"It didn't do any good," Maureen said. "There are thousands of people still goin' to gawk."

"Yes," Jacob agreed, "but Rose gave a few of them something to think about. Gussie always said you win people over one at a time."

"Is Gussie's union hall near here?" I asked.

Jacob nodded. "The Waistmakers Local 25 on Clinton Street."

"I want to see it."

When we reached Clinton Street, it wasn't hard tellin'

which building housed the union. It was draped in black from top to bottom.

"I'd like to stay here alone for a while," I said.

Maureen touched my arm. "Are ye all right, Rose?"

I nodded. I could feel the tears fillin' my eyes.

"I'll go back with Maureen," Jacob said. "I want to pay my respects to Mr. Garoff." He started to move away, then stopped to look at me. "I just can't believe . . ." He choked on the words and shook his head.

Maureen took his hand. "I know, Jacob. I know." She turned to me. "Take as long as you need, Rose."

"Thank you," I whispered, feelin' empty inside. I went to stand across the street from the union hall. So this was where Gussie had spent so much of her time—this sad place dressed in black like a widow. I watched people goin' in and out. I could tell that many of them were families of the girls who had died.

I started thinkin' about what lay ahead for me. First of all, Maureen and I would have to find another place to stay, now that Mr. Garoff was goin' back to Russia. Later today we would go to Uncle Patrick to let him know what had happened. We'd need to send a telegram to Da and Ma right away. Even if they hadn't received my letter yet, they would in the next few days, and they'd be sick with worry, knowin' that I worked at the Triangle. Word of the fire had probably reached Europe already.

As I watched the heavy black fabric flap in the wind,

I remembered the day Gussie made me stand up to Moscovitz. We won that battle, but it was only a small one. Moscovitz might have cheated his girls out of a few dollars and stolen a few kisses, but the owners of the Triangle stole the lives of one hundred forty-six people. I had never seen those men or heard their names, but they had held my fate in their hands without me even knowin' it. And they had let my friends die.

This time when I got a job, I'd join the union and work in a union shop, where somebody would be lookin' out for me. Gussie had been right about that. And Maureen wouldn't be workin' at all. She'd stay in school until she was sixteen. I wouldn't let her talk me out of it again.

I'd save up for visits back to Limerick. I couldn't bear the thought of never seein' my family again. Da and Ma would always be in my heart, but I was a grown woman now, not somebody's little girl. The fire had changed me. Like a piece of iron in a blacksmith's forge, I had come out reshaped, stronger. I no longer feared foolish things like walkin' Thomond Bridge alone at night, for I had faced somethin' far more terrible than a ghost, and I had survived.

I had the same feelin' as when I first jumped for the swingin' rope at Boys Sandy. It had taken courage to fling myself out on the air, prayin' I'd be able to grab hold. That same courage had saved me in the fire, and it would save me now. I was goin' to reach out and grab this new life in America with all my strength, because I was brought here for a purpose. Gussie Garoff, Rose Klein, Rose Bellini, and all the others were silent now, so it was up to girls like me to make sure they weren't forgotten. There was a lot that needed to be said about what had happened at the Triangle Shirtwaist Company.

And I was goin' to tell everybody who would listen.

Author's Note

🌹 *I was first drawn* to the story of the Triangle fire by the PBS *New York* documentary. The pictures from the fire haunted me for several months before I decided to write about it. I started out with the common misconception that many of the Triangle workers were Irish. Since my grandmother Margaret Nolan Springer had sailed to New York from Ireland in the late nineteenth century, I gave her maiden name to the mother of the main character. My grandmother had come to this country to work as a maid for a German family, later marrying one of the sons. So I wrote the early chapters of the book, bringing the Nolan family through Ellis Island to settle with Uncle Patrick's German family in New York.

Then I found the victim list from the fire. As I read through the Russian, Polish, and Italian names, I was ready to discard my first chapters and have the main characters be one of those nationalities. When I discovered "Dorrity, Anna—Irish immigrant" on the list, I knew I could keep my Irish Rose, for her isolation would be more poignant if she were living outside of her culture. In studying the victim list, I found that "Rose" was the most common name.

There Is an Isle, by Criostoir O'Flynn, gave me wonderful details of a Limerick childhood on the Island Parish. This book, along with the photographs in *Through Irish Eyes,* published by Smithmark, allowed me to picture the life Rose had left behind in Ireland.

I read many accounts of Ellis Island, but it was a visit to the restored landmark that helped me to experience how it must have been when the Nolan family saw America for the first time. One thing not described in any of the books was the semicircular window in the registry room, which frames New York as if the city were a huge painting.

During the course of my research, I visited the George Eastman House in Rochester, New York, where assistant archivist Joseph Struble showed me the Lewis W. Hine photo collection. Here I was able to see faces of factory workers from the period and even a flower-making sweatshop that became the model for Moscovitz's shop in the book.

There are many resources available about the fire itself, but I found *The Triangle Fire,* by Leon Stein, to be the most complete. Through newspaper articles from the days following the fire and interviews with survivors, he gives a minute-by-minute account of the fire and a vivid picture of a stunned and grieving city. Though out of print for a number of years, the book has been newly released in paperback.

I also located a wealth of information and devastating photographs on the comprehensive Web site presented by the Kheel Center for Labor-Management Documentation and Archives at Cornell University. *The Historical Atlas of New York City,* by Eric Homberger, was valuable in showing me the location of subways, tenements, and ethnic neighborhoods from the period.

In piecing together what Rose's life might have been like, I found *Ladies of Labor, Girls of Adventure,* by Nan Enstad, to be a fascinating resource, telling about the dime novels, the nickelodeons, and the political implications of fashions popular with working girls of the period. This, along with some accounts from survivors, led me to believe that, though the hours were long, the work was tedious, and the building was unsafe, many of the Triangle girls probably had enjoyed the camaraderie with fellow workers, unaware of the devastation that awaited them.

In April 1911, Max Blanck and Isaac Harris, the owners of the Triangle Waist Company, were indicted on charges of first- and second-degree manslaughter on the grounds that the locked doors had trapped their workers. They were later acquitted of those charges, because the jury couldn't determine that they had ordered the doors to be locked. Blanck and Harris, known as the "shirtwaist kings," continued in the garment industry, ignoring the welfare of their workers.

But from the ashes of the Triangle fire rose a stronger labor movement. Some of the first worker-safety laws were a direct result of the anger generated by the fire and the acquittal of the owners, as legislators vowed not to let such a tragedy happen again.

On the day I delivered this manuscript to my editor, the last survivor of the Triangle fire died. Her name was Rose— Rose Rosenfeld Freedman. She was not quite eighteen at the time of the fire and lived to the age of 107. Throughout her life she crusaded for worker safety, telling the story of the fire again and again at labor rallies. A year before her death, Rose Freedman said this in the PBS documentary *The Living Century:* "To me, 106 is a number. I lived that long, not only on account of my genes, but on account of my attitude. You've got to stand up for yourself. Am I right?"